IT TAKES TWO TO STRANGLE

A Damon Lassard Dabbling Detective Mystery

by

Stephen Kaminski

For information, email **Cozy Cat Press**, cozycatpress@aol.com or visit our website at: www.cozycatpress.com

ISBN: 978-0-9881943-1-1
Printed in the United States of America

Cover design by Karri Klawiter
http://artbykarri.wordpress.com

1 2 3 4 5 6 7 8 9 10

Dedication: To Amy and Maya

Chapter 1

Damon Lassard bounced on the balls of his feet in time to the pulse of evening traffic. Standing at the crosswalk in front of his local grocer, he smiled to himself. He had convinced the manager to donate twelve dozen hamburgers for the upcoming Fourth of July picnic. The modest feat would free enough funds for the Hollydale Citizens Association to rent the county's clown-inspired moon bounce—something his predecessor as president had never managed. Not that Damon cared to impress anyone, other than his mother and Bethany Krims. Damon shook his head. The chance of Bethany coming to a local fireworks party was almost non-existent. Given her current love interest and his connections, she would doubtless attend a demonstrably more upscale gathering.

The light changed and gears audibly ground to a halt on the street in front of him. Damon crossed and turned down the block toward Rebecca Leeds' storefront cooking school. Hollydale's primary business route teemed with commuters, but the wide clean sidewalk was largely devoid of pedestrians at six o'clock on a Monday.

Damon poked his head in the door of "The Cookery."

"Anything good left Rebecca?" he shouted over the pounding of an industrial-sized dishwasher.

Rebecca cut the light streaming through the front windows with her hand and visibly brightened. "There are a few pieces of pie on the counter, but none of mine." She swatted at dark brown bangs.

He stepped inside and eyed the student creations. The smell of fresh dough tickled his nostrils.

Rebecca flicked down a glowing green switch on the dishwasher and its angry hammering subsided to a low growl. "There's some pecan and apple-rhubarb left," she said. "But I wouldn't touch the pecan. Mrs. Chenworth made that one and it'll take you hours to scrape the goo off the roof of your mouth."

Damon pictured Mrs. Chenworth's large frame shaking with fervor as she poured puddles of caramel into her crust so no one could interrupt one of her diatribes. "Can I finish the apple-rhubarb?" he asked.

"Absolutely." Rebecca slid her athletic legs over a tall stool in front of the narrow stainless steel countertop. "I'm exhausted. I've been on the phone for the past hour with my credit card company. Someone stole my card this afternoon."

Damon raised his eyebrows.

"Whoever took it didn't steal my handbag," she continued. "I had no idea the card was even gone until I received a call asking if I charged four hundred dollars to a clothing store fifty miles from here."

"Are you sure you didn't leave it somewhere?"

Rebecca crinkled her nose. "Yes, I'm sure."

Rebecca was still on the southern tip of thirty and many men found her tiny nose, pouty smile and tomboy figure attractive. But Damon never felt a physical connection in her presence. He speculated that was the reason they had become such fast friends. Whether Rebecca had any interest in Damon, she never let on as far as he could tell. Of course, he was much better at figuring out when a woman had no interest in him.

"Do you have any idea what happened?" he asked.

"I think so. I went downtown this morning to a cookware show at the convention center. Afterwards, I stopped for lunch at a deli counter." She pushed palms against bare knees. "It was packed and I had to wait for a table. The first seat that freed up was wedged against the back of a chair at another table. I made the mistake of hanging my bag over my chair."

"And someone reached in and took out your credit card."

"I was sitting back to back with the woman behind me. My handbag was practically in her lap." Damon smiled at her through a mouthful of rhubarb. "I think she took the whole wallet out, because less than two minutes after I sat down she pushed up against me and went off to the bathroom."

"So she went to the bathroom, took out the credit card out and slipped your wallet back into your bag when she sat back down," Damon said.

"Exactly. I had about thirty dollars in cash, but she didn't touch it. My credit card was behind my driver's license, so even if I had opened my wallet, I wouldn't have noticed until the next time I needed to use the card."

"That's a pretty smart move on her part," Damon said. "That way she could use it and toss it before you even knew it was gone."

Damon leaned into the counter across from Rebecca, picked up the remaining pie crust with his fingers and held his head over the pan while he chewed the buttery shell.

Rebecca rose and unleashed a shower of spray from a bottled cleaner onto the other end of countertop. She stepped over to the misted surface and scrubbed vigorously with a folded paper towel.

Rebecca had been one of the first people Damon befriended after moving to Hollydale two years earlier.

His mother insisted that he take cooking classes on the pretext that his intake of restaurant fare and her leftovers couldn't last. Their friendship blossomed immediately.

"It's a pain in the neck to shut down the card, but I haven't even told you the most frustrating part," Rebecca said. She stopped scrubbing. "Not only did the woman who took my card buy four hundred plus dollars of clothes, but she made a charitable donation."

"She did what?"

"There's a five hundred dollar charge to an organization that funds cancer treatments for children in Central America."

Damon smiled despite himself. "So the thief makes up for her transgressions by performing a selfless act?"

"It's pretty easy to be altruistic with someone else's money." Rebecca finished wiping the counter and sat back down.

"I'm sure the credit card company will remove the charge," Damon said.

"The woman on the phone said all I have to do is dispute the charges I didn't make with their claims department. But I don't know if I can bring myself to fight a donation to help needy kids with cancer."

"You looked at their website didn't you?"

Rebecca flushed. "Yes. A five hundred dollar donation provides six months of treatment for a toddler. How can I take that away now?"

Damon picked at his teeth. "You just have to rationalize it. I'm sure the charity hasn't sent the money along yet and it probably hasn't even been earmarked for a particular child."

"I know, but it's churning my insides. I can't exactly afford to make a five hundred dollar donation right now. But I wouldn't lose my home or business if I just left it alone. I'm stuck between my conscience and my bank account." She breathed loudly. "Sorry to vent, Damon. But I needed to tell someone."

"I'm glad you did. Don't do anything yet. How long do you have to dispute the charge?"

"Thirty days."

"Let's both think on it for a couple of days." Damon stretched his back muscles. "I have some good news. I just convinced Doc Marley over at the Safeway to open up his coffers and supply burgers for the Fourth of July party."

"That's wonderful, Damon. I didn't think you could top last year, but I have a feeling you'll find a way."

"I hope so. I saw someone from the county mowing the grass on the ridge yesterday, so it should be in good condition as long as we don't get too much rain."

As a small community in Arlington, Virginia—less than three miles west of Washington, D.C.—Hollydale had the luxury of sitting on a ridge that overlooked the city. While the view along the crest was breathtaking in the winter months, during the balance of the year, trees in full bloom crowded the vista from every vantage point other than the county picnic facility in Hollydale. Every July, crowds of neighbors funneled to the spot to watch the fireworks rise over the Potomac River.

"I'm just finishing up here," Rebecca said. "Do you want to join me for dinner?"

"Sorry, I was just passing by and wanted to stop in for a treat. I'm heading off to meet with Liz de la Cruz and the carnival owners. They start set-up for the county fair first thing tomorrow morning. Between the fair starting on Wednesday and the Fourth of July party on Friday, this week is crazy for me." Damon sighed. "And on top of everything else, after my meeting tonight, I promised my mother I'd finish re-grouting her shower." He saw Rebecca stifle a snicker.

"No problem," Rebecca said and switched the dishwasher back to full hammering mode. She gave him a grin over her shoulder, ignoring the dirty pie tin Damon left on the counter as he exited.

Liz de la Cruz was Damon's citizens association counterpart in neighboring Oakwood. Because the county fairgrounds spread over their two communities—the athletic fields at Wickland Elementary School in Hollydale and barren pasture in Oakwood—the Arlington County commissioner asked Damon and Liz to serve as point personnel for the upcoming fair. That included meeting with Big Surf Shows, the new carnival operator.

Damon pulled into the elementary school parking and saw Liz liberally applying cherry Carmex. The woman used more lip balm than anyone Damon had ever met.

They walked downhill to a metallic blue pick-up parked in the schoolyard between a baseball diamond and the edge of farmland. The grounds were ideal for a fair—fifteen acres of relatively flat and treeless land.

A man in his early fifties with sparse black hair clinging to its final days watched them approach. Broken capillaries around his eyes betrayed a drinking habit. He wore a faux Burberry-checked long sleeve shirt under a tan hunting vest and slightly worn jeans despite a temperature in the mid-eighties.

The man reached out a meaty hand starting to spot with age. "Lirim Jovanović. My partner Jim Riley and I own Big Surf." He had a slight Slavic accent and directed his introduction to Damon, but eyed Liz with leering appreciation. Liz was oblivious.

"Damon Lassard from Hollydale and this is Liz de la Cruz from Oakwood," Damon said. "What do you think of the grounds?"

"They look pretty good. There's already a good-sized parking lot at the school so we don't have to put one on the grass and there's plenty of open space so the generator fumes shouldn't be a problem."

"Generator fumes?" interrupted Liz.

Lirim rolled his eyes toward Damon but responded patiently. "If we didn't use generators, we'd have to run electrical lines across the fairgrounds and up to the school. You wouldn't want that, would you?"

"I guess not," Liz said quietly.

"Here's a rough outline of the set-up," Lirim said. He set a legal-sized notepad on the hood of his truck and showed them blocks marked for rides, games, concessions and motorized trailers that served as living quarters for the traveling workers. Damon caught a whiff of whiskey when he leaned in for a closer look and realized it was exuding from Lirim's pores.

Lirim looked up at the sound of approaching footsteps and his complexion darkened. He introduced his partner Jim Riley to Damon and Liz through gritted teeth.

Jim was a small man with a clean-shaven goatee and a somewhat bulbous reddening on one of his earlobes. It looked more infected than sunburned. Liz eyed it curiously. Damon fancied that she wanted to soothe it with a heavy dollop of Carmex.

The muscles tensed in Jim's neck when he spoke. He explained that he had been measuring land gradients to assess water flow which tended to cause large muddy areas when masses of people congregated on a low spot. They'd make sure to keep the most popular attractions away from the low lying land.

Liz asked a few more questions and Damon agreed to meet the carnival owners at the same spot the following morning when the entire carnival rolled into town.

Damon parked at the curb next to his mother's modern townhouse in Hollydale. The community was an eclectic mix of old and new. Pre-fab homes from the early 1900s for the working-class were slowly giving way to large, vertical houses as the older ones fell into disrepair and were sold. The people living in Hollydale largely mirrored their houses. Those occupying older homes were typically long-time residents and the majority of the new houses were occupied by the endless supply of transplanted lobbyists and management consultants who lived in Hollydale, but tended to shop and eat in downtown D.C.

Damon considered his mother's brick townhouse. The prospect of living on four levels, so narrow that a third of the floor space was taken up by stairs, didn't appeal to him. But his mother never complained— Lynne Lassard-Brown had lived there for six years, including three since her second husband Jack passed away.

A rolling filing cabinet with colored paper bursting from the drawers greeted Damon as he pushed through the unlocked burgundy and brass front door.

"Mother, I'm here," he shouted, skirting the filing cabinet only to be met by a three-foot-wide gold frame leaning against the sitting room loveseat.

"I'm in the kitchen, Damon."

Damon deftly steered past dining room and kitchen clutter and kissed his mother on the cheek.

"That's awfully chipper for someone who's about to spend a couple of hours on his knees in my shower," said Lynne, posing cross-legged on a spindled kitchen chair. Her graying blond hair swirled into a nest piled atop her head, showing off a graceful neckline. Damon had to give his mother credit: she kept in better shape than almost anyone he knew—it must be all of those stairs.

"I'm happy to see you looking so good mother," Damon said.

She ignored the compliment. "I saw Bethany Krims today," Lynne said and moved to pour Damon a cup of coffee.

"You know Bethany has never shown the slightest interest in me," Damon replied and reached for the steaming mug his mother extended.

"I know. Which is why I don't understand why you don't start taking your relationship with Rebecca to the next level."

Damon frowned and reversed course. "So where did you see Bethany?"

"Down at Cynthia's." Cynthia, who doubled as Damon's citizens association vice president, owned a salon next door to Rebecca's cooking school. The salon was doing its best to rival an old-fashioned barber shop as a place for exchanging information among Hollydale's local women.

"Mrs. Chenworth asked her how serious she was with that attorney she's been dating," Lynne said. "Bethany told her they had parted company."

Damon's heart lurched, although he knew it was baseless. Bethany had been single on several occasions since Damon moved to Hollydale, but it hadn't increased his chances with her. Not that he had ever summoned the courage to ask her out.

Two flights upstairs, Damon laid out the repair materials he had purchased earlier in the week and dug into the project for his widowed mother. Lynne met Jack while he was on a business trip to Michigan six and a half years earlier. Within months they were married and she moved from a quaint suburb of Detroit into Jack's townhome in Hollydale. Damon was overseas at the time and only met Jack once before the wedding.

Damon spent seven years as a baseball player in Japan. After college, he knew he wouldn't cut it as a professional in the States, so he moved sight unseen across the globe. He caught on with a farm club in Kyoto because they had a knuckleball pitcher and few players could catch a knuckleballer like Damon. When the pitcher, Masaso Kimura, was called up to the major leagues, he insisted that Damon be given a contract.

Despite his limited batting skills, it was during Damon's tenure with the Hokkaido Nippon-Ham Fighters in Sapporo that he made enough money to be comfortably off. Damon had been in a one-for-fifteen slump, but on a windy Saturday afternoon, he connected with a fastball and drove it into the outfield corner. The ball took a strange ricochet off the back wall, allowing Damon to round the bases for his first ever inside-the-park home run. As he crossed home plate, Masaso ran out from the dugout and embraced Damon in an enormous bear hug.

The seemingly innocent gesture between the Japanese and American players caught the attention of a fan-favorite national sportscaster, and the next thing Damon and Masaso knew, they were cast as the poster boys of Kushiro Chewing Gum's latest ad campaign. He didn't consider himself exceptionally good looking, but his clear blue eyes occasionally drew him a second glance.

Once the Japanese public tired of seeing Damon and Masaso, and Damon was relegated to the minor leagues, he decided it was time to return to the States. Given the recent death of his mother's second husband, Damon knew that she would appreciate the presence of her only child. He moved into an updated duplex three streets over from Lynne Lassard-Brown's townhouse.

Damon knew he was in a unique situation. At thirty-one years of age, given his relatively frugal spending habits and chewing gum money, he didn't actually have to get a job. Instead, at Rebecca's suggestion, he volunteered at the Hollydale branch library. Damon wasn't an avid reader, but this suggestion had appealed to him on two fronts. He could volunteer on a part-time basis and Bethany Krims spent a significant amount of time there.

"Have you eaten dinner yet, Damon?" Lynne asked, resting a hip against the inside of the bathroom doorframe.

"Rebecca let me have some leftover pie at The Cookery, so I'm fine."

Lynne pushed aside a half dozen plastic razors and placed a bowl of Bing cherries on the bathroom vanity. "So how's Rebecca?"

Damon scoured grout-laden hands under cool sink water. "She's fine, except someone stole her credit card this afternoon." He filled his mother in.

"That's terrible," Lynne said, nibbling on the end of a cherry stem. "I remember when your father was still alive, Damon. After I first starting using a credit card, he would tease me incessantly. He'd say 'I wish someone would steal your purse, Lynne. I'm sure the thief would spend less than you do.'"

She laughed. Damon dried his hands and wrapped his arms around his mother's sinuous body. Her warmth passed through him and he tightened his squeeze. Losing two husbands hadn't been easy for her.

She broke away. A small tear trickled down her cheek and she hastily wiped it away.

Damon picked up her signal. "So mother, how did you manage to get nail polish in between the shower tiles?"

Ignoring the playful jab, Lynne kissed him lightly on the forehead and started down the stairs. "You're going to give Rebecca five hundred dollars to cover the thief's gift," she said. It was a statement rather than a question. It gave Damon great comfort that she knew him so well.

Chapter 2

The following morning, a Tuesday, Damon arrived
at the fairgrounds to meet the carnival caravan. He had
taken the week off from his volunteer duties at the
library to focus on the carnival and that Friday's Fourth
of July picnic. The temperature was expected to hover
in the eighties but Bethany, who was the weatherperson
for the evening news at one of the northern Virginia
broadcast stations, had forecast a chance of rain later in
the week.

Two dozen massive vehicles stampeded through the
elementary school parking lot, gingerly down the
adjacent grassy slope and onto the fairgrounds. Damon
jogged after the parade. Lirim Jovanović climbed down
from the lead trailer and shook Damon's hand. He wore
the same tan hunting vest and jeans and his pores gave
off the same scent.

Lirim introduced Damon to a heavyset man in his
mid-forties who pounded the ground with his feet when
he walked. Victor McElroy was the carnival's self-
entitled "money man" because he collected every dollar
that came in and paid out every employee at the end of
the week, all in cash. He also doubled as the fair's pig
racing announcer. Victor's wide shoulders dwarfed his
head and huge hands bore fingernails chewed to the
nubs. His pallid complexion and scowl formed a
boorish duet.

"If you have any trouble with anything, you don't
need to bother Mr. Jovanović or Mr. Riley, just come to

me," Victor told Damon, glancing quickly at Lirim as he spoke.

Damon replied noncommittally, excused himself and re-climbed the hill to join Cynthia who had decided that her role as citizens association vice president entitled her to a peek at the carnival crew's set-up.

Cynthia was a classic underachiever, but Damon liked her well enough. She inherited the salon five years earlier when her mother gracefully moved on to Hollydale's assisted living center. But unlike her mother, Cynthia didn't cut hair or paint nails. Rather, she spent countless hours every afternoon making sure the ladies of Hollydale had a bantering partner.

They spent a solid half hour in relative silence perched on the hood of Damon's Saab, staring out at the transformation of the fairgrounds. Enormous metal structures were slowly being manipulated by teams of shirtless men into shapes that became recognizable as the Tilt-a-Whirl, the Scrambler and a massive Funhouse.

When two men started to unload stand-up video games onto dollies, Cynthia declared that everything looked to be in order and she was heading to the salon.

Damon strolled to the arcade tent where Jim Riley was talking to a gangly kid who stood six foot three and was as skinny as one of the poles holding up the tent. Jim introduced him as Skipper.

"Skipper might be young, but he's a technical godsend," Jim said. "He's taking engineering classes at George Mason and fixes all of our electronics and hydraulics. Let me tell you, this kid is going to be my meal ticket to bigger things."

Skipper reddened, but smiled.

Damon wondered what Skipper thought of being Jim Riley's meal ticket, but asked Skipper instead, "Are you planning to stay with Big Surf or move on once you have your degree?"

"I want to design roller coasters," Skipper said with a dreamy look.

Jim wandered away and Damon watched Skipper plug in a giant "Claw Machine" game. He used a key from a hulking chain dangling from his belt to open the front panel.

"Want to know how one of these works?" Skipper asked in a friendly manner, looking back over his shoulder.

"What do you mean? Don't you just center the claw over the stuffed animal and try to grab it?"

"Nope. I control it right here with this little yellow box. Have you ever noticed how someone will have a toy in the claw and it's moving upward and then all of a sudden, the claw just opens and the toy falls out?"

"Sure," Damon admitted. "I just thought the grip wasn't good enough."

"Not the case. It's the win-setting that I control with this box. If I position it to ten, the claw will hold on tightly to every tenth grab and let go of the other nine."

"Really," Damon said, a bit surprised. "That seems a little unfair."

"I guess. But that's the way these things are designed. If you ever want to win, just find yourself a nice inconspicuous spot to watch the machine. Count how many drops there are between wins and there you go. During the next cycle, wait out the drops and move in to play the game right before the next scheduled win." Skipper beamed with his inside knowledge.

Despite his complicity in the Claw Game scheme, Damon decided he liked Skipper and his easygoing temperament.

Damon heard his name and looked up to see Gerry Sloman raise his hand in a wave. Damon bid Skipper farewell and made his way over to the Arlington County detective. Gerry was another person Damon genuinely liked. He was only a few years older than Damon and despite his determined nature, he had an appealing sense of integrity and a refreshingly understated air. Damon found his role as community police liaison more interesting than any other part of his job as citizens association president. Gerry, who had recently been promoted to detective, was his primary contact with the police.

A small gold cross dangled from Gerry's neck. He was the only person Damon had ever known who converted from Judaism to Catholicism.

"What's going on Detective?" Damon asked as he shook Gerry's hand.

"I owe a favor to a friend in the commissioner's office and he decided to cash it in. I have some paperwork for the carnival management to fill out. Any idea who that is?"

"I do," Damon said. "There are two owners, Jim Riley and Lirim Jovanović. Let's see if we can track them down."

Damon led Gerry to the far back edge of the fairgrounds. A line of silver trailers stood side by side like sardines in a newly opened can.

He asked a panting woman in a leopard-print skirt who was carrying an overstuffed laundry sack if she knew which coaches belonged to Lirim and Jim.

She pointed to a coach near the center of the line. "Mr. Riley shares that one with three other people. Mr. Jovanović has the trailer at the end." She moved her finger and directed it to the trailer closest to the elementary school. "He keeps it all to himself. Everybody else is four to a trailer, but he doesn't like noise. He says he needs his peace to run things." Her facial expression and tone suggested that she didn't care for Lirim's managerial style.

Damon and Gerry tried Jim's trailer first without success. They strode to Lirim's trailer at the end of the row, and Gerry rapped sharply.

"Don't bother me now," Lirim bellowed.

"Police here. I have some papers I need you to sign and I'm not coming back," Gerry retorted.

"Hold on," Lirim said. Twenty seconds later, the coach door swung open and Lirim brusquely waved them inside. They entered and Victor McElroy stood up from a table, shoving stacks of receipts into a large manila envelope.

Damon introduced Gerry to the men.

Lirim forced a smile. "Won't you two gentlemen have a seat while I just have a last word outside with my accounts manager."

Damon glanced around the inside of the coach. It was worn with years of hard living. Cigarette burns pockmarked the linoleum floor and a stained pea green two-seater sofa worn to the springs pushed up against a side wall. On the back wall stood a cramped kitchen area consisting of a narrow refrigerator devoid of embellishment, an electric cook-top range caked with grease and a scratched microwave oven. Across from the kitchen, the single upright wooden chair where Victor had been sitting was wedged under a scuffed table. Around a partial wall Damon could make out a bedroom, but it was dark.

Gerry took the chair at the table, which was a good move. If pressed to sit, Damon would be stuck on the sofa with its mystery stains.

Lirim returned and impressed a jocular attitude. "Sorry about the wait. Victor and I were just going through the receipts from last week's fair in Burke Woods."

While Gerry and Lirim tended to a half-inch stack of papers, Damon excused himself and stepped outside for a breath of fresh air. Descending the two front stairs, he saw Victor open a back door to the trailer next door— less than fifteen feet away. Victor tossed the manila envelope inward and kicked the door closed behind him.

Damon planned to meet Rebecca at the Fish Barrel in Hollydale for dinner that evening. The restaurant was housed in an attractive red-brick building along Hollydale's main commercial street. Aided by an open architecture and tables made from a charming variety of finished knotty woods, it was neither pretentious nor tacky.

Damon arrived before Rebecca and was seated at a table directly facing a striking couple sitting across from one another. He was a lean, clean-cut black man in his early thirties hunched forward trying to impress a point. She was Eastern European with a mien that could best be described as sultry. Her dark features were rough and sensual, and she had a raw aura that emanated sexual hunger.

Damon ran his hand over the small widow's peak touching down in the center of his forehead. He once looked up the term and had been horrified to see a list of famous widow's peaks topped by Eddie Munster and Richard Nixon.

He felt a momentary wave of intensity and realized that the dark haired, dark eyed woman at the table across from him had torn her gaze away from her companion and settled her sights briefly on him. As soon as the feeling had come, it passed as she swept her eyes around the restaurant.

Moments later, Rebecca joined him. Damon pushed a check for five hundred dollars across the table to cover the credit card thief's donation. He held a finger to his lips and wouldn't allow Rebecca to refuse it.

They ordered nachos to share and shortly after the food arrived, Damon managed to singe his wrist in scalding cheese. He quickly sucked away the burning sensation and Rebecca launched into a rant about Cynthia's salon. Cynthia continually placed her trash bins behind The Cookery rather than at the back of the salon. When the garbage collectors inevitably dropped heaps of trash while loading it onto their truck, the refuse wound up in front of Rebecca's back door.

At a lull, Damon said, "When I was younger I wanted to be a trash collector." He paused. "I thought they only worked on Thursdays."

"Hilarious," Rebecca responded but she had a smile stretching between her dimples.

The restaurant's front door swung open and Lirim Jovanović appeared, trailed by Victor McElroy. Lirim had replaced the hunting vest with a dark green polo short, but hadn't changed his jeans.

Neither man noticed Damon, and Lirim's eyes fixed on the nearby couple. Lirim approached the table and said callously, "Hello, Clara."

The woman remained seated. "Hello father, you remember Jordan."

The neatly dressed Jordan stood and extended his hand. Lirim shook it after a slight pause and took a seat at their table. "You remember my accountant Victor, don't you, dear?" Lirim said directing his words toward Clara, and intoning "dear" as a euphemism.

"How are you, Victor?" replied Clara with equal coldness and introduced Jordan. Victor declined to shake Jordan's hand and wedged his square, but muscular, frame into the last remaining seat.

"To what do I owe the honor of a personal meeting with you and the good doctor here in Arlington?" Lirim asked. This time, he managed to make the word "doctor" sound like an insult.

"We're staying at the Sheraton here for a few days and I need my money," Clara said without preface. "Probate on Mom's will finished three months ago and you've been holding back what's rightfully mine."

"There are some legal complications, Clara."

"That's bull. Mom's accident was a year and a half ago and I know for a fact that Uncle Toma already received his share."

"Your situation is different than Toma's, and stop shouting," countered Lirim. He noticed Damon sitting just feet away.

Damon tried to shift his eyes to Rebecca, but not before Lirim saw him focused on their table. Lirim lifted his hand weakly in Damon's direction.

Damon gave him a nod and the conversation at Lirim's table swung to hushed tones.

"I wonder what kind of accident she had," whispered Rebecca after Damon filled her in that Lirim was one of the carnival owners. Damon imagined a giant claw plucking a woman from the fairgrounds and just as she reached the height of the Ferris wheel, it opened its grip and sent the woman plummeting downward.

After they finished their meal, Damon obliged the manners his mother had instilled in him and stopped at Lirim's table. The carnival operator treated Rebecca to the same unctuous once-over he had given Liz de la Cruz. Rebecca suppressed a shudder. Lirim introduced them to Clara and to her boyfriend, Jordan Hall.

Clara stood to meet Damon and he felt a spasm below his waist. Her full lips mouthed a tranquil "hello." It took all of his efforts not to let his eyes follow their way down to her breasts, especially after internally chastising Lirim for doing just that to Rebecca. Clara seemed to instinctively read his thoughts and shifted her hips to wickedly draw his eyes to the curves tugging at her Capri pants.

"You have arresting blue eyes, Mr. Lassard," she said bluntly and gave his outstretched hand a delicate shake, letting the tips of her fingernails graze his wrist. Noticing the intimate gesture, Jordan stood abruptly and proffered a handshake of his own to cut off the interlude.

"Damon is helping with the standard red tape here in town," Lirim told the group as Clara swiveled back into her chair. "My daughter Clara here never really was one for the carnival business. She thinks she can make a better living roping in doctors like Jordan here."

Clara frowned.

"She's actually one of the best geriatric nurses the hospital has Mr. Jovanović," Jordan said.

Rebecca stepped into the middle of the family argument and asked Jordan, "Do you and Clara work at the same hospital?"

Jordan turned grateful eyes to Rebecca and nodded. "Yes. We're both at St. Michael's outside of Richmond. She works in one of the upstairs wings. I'm down in the Emergency Room."

"Are you going to make it to the fair?" Rebecca asked.

"I'm not sure," Jordan said. "We're just in town to see some friends and take care of some family business."

They bantered for another minute while the tension cooled. Victor sat stolidly and Lirim glared at his daughter who picked at her food. Damon forced himself to wish them a pleasant evening before he and Rebecca escaped.

"Be careful of that one," Rebecca said as they stepped through the patio to the sidewalk.

"Which one?"

"I meant Clara. I saw the way she hooked your attention. But I guess Lirim and his silent bodyguard-accountant warrant some caution, too."

"I suppose," Damon replied, "but they'll all be out of town by Sunday."

They made their way toward the Hollydale's residential district in a comfortable silence, and Damon's thoughts drifted to the movement of Clara's hips. Hers was a sexuality very unlike Bethany's. Clara was physical and raw. Bethany was refined. He peeked sideways at Rebecca and wished he felt the same internal stirring for her, but it just wasn't there.

When Damon arrived home, his duplex neighbor was sitting on their shared front porch per his usual evening routine. David Einstaff poured Damon a tumbler of whiskey and ashed his cigarette. "So what do you think about this business with your mother?" David inquired in his low drawling voice.

A fifty-something father of three, David was recently divorced. As far as Damon could glean in the few months since David moved in, his neighbor went to work six days a week in a suit, didn't like to talk about his job and enjoyed his evenings outside with whiskey and more than a few cigarettes.

Damon plunked down in the chair beside David's. "What business about my mother is that?"

"Just that she was getting herself dolled up over at Cynthia's this afternoon," he said taking a sip from his glass. "Mrs. Chenworth stopped me at the Safeway. Seeing as how you and I are neighbors, she figured that I was just dying to know that Lynne Lassard-Brown might be headed somewhere special on a Tuesday night."

Damon's mother was about the same age as David, if not a year or two younger, and Damon wouldn't put it past David to have an interest in her. Most men in the fifty and above set did. "I guess I'll have to ask her about it," Damon said. "Or maybe I should just find Mrs. Chenworth. I'm sure she'll know."

Later that evening, Damon called his mother and quizzed her.

"Now how in the world do you know about that?" she asked.

"Mrs. Chenworth was telling anyone who would care to listen that you were making yourself even prettier than usual at Cynthia's earlier today."

"Well it's no secret," she said. "Charles Swickley took me to a steakhouse in Georgetown."

"Charles Swickley? He must be pushing eighty!"

"Seventy-two and so what? It was nice to dress up and go out on the town for once."

"Mother, there are countless men who would take you out. And it's not as if they ever stop asking you. What made you say yes to Swickley?"

"Do you really want to know?" she asked demurely.

"I do."

"I thought I could have a nice dinner out without having to worry about him trying to get into my pants at the end of the night."

Damon groaned.

"Well," she said. "Don't you want to know if he tried?"

The county fair opened for business the following evening. Walking through the entryway marked by a pair of poles dressed in colorful flags, Damon was hit by an avalanche of carnival scents. The combination of funnel cakes, cotton candy and corn dogs sent his olfactory glands into overdrive. A row of vendor trucks—the original "food trucks"— staffed by fresh faced youths lined the front right side of the grounds. To the left of the entrance stood the exhibition pavilion. Directly in front of him stretched a vast labyrinth of carnival games and rides flanked on its outer edges by a pig-racing course on one side and an outdoor amphitheatre on the other. The amphitheatre would host puppet shows and magicians during the day, live auctions in the early evening and local bands at night.

Damon meandered through a warren of skee-ball, whack-a-mole, and pop-a-shot games. He saw a father curse under his breath at the giant claw as a stuffed dolphin slipped out of its grasp and a four-year-old girl shrieked in dismay. Emerging from the flashing lights and crush of carnival workers touting the glory of balloon dart and shoot-the-star winners, Damon rested his eyes on the largest of the rides. The Matterhorn, Gravitron and Zipper might look small in a commercial amusement park, but here, at the fairgrounds, they loomed like giants.

He cut through a line forming for the derelict "haunted house" and spotted Bethany Krims nibbling the hardened exterior of a cherry-dipped ice cream cone. Wavy chestnut hair bobbed at her shoulders. She was alone, but scanning the crowd. Damon took a deep breath and approached.

"Hi, Bethany. How's the ice cream?"

"Oh, hi, Damon. It's pretty good."

"I might have to get one myself pretty soon. No weather forecast tonight?"

"Thankfully, I get Wednesdays off," she replied, swatting at a fly that made a beeline for her cone. She bent her head to lick a bit of vanilla that had run down the backside.

"Do you want to take a ride on the Matterhorn?" Damon asked nervously.

She held up her cone. "Sorry." The mild gesture made Damon feel as if he had just been eliminated in the first round of a grade school spelling contest.

Before he could stammer out a reply, she waved excitedly past him and a gangling woman with heavy eyebrows rushed forward. The two women gushed over each other for a few moments. Bethany quickly introduced Damon to her cousin Laura and the two women walked off arm-in-arm toward the exhibition pavilion.

Victor McElroy's voice boomed through a megaphone over the crowd, announcing the upcoming pig races. Damon purchased a greasy cardboard cup of waffle fries and headed over to the racing stands.

From a makeshift press box, Victor shouted out the names of the entrants in the first heat, along with a colorful commentary of each pig's racing prowess. The lines were well scripted for comedic value, stock-in-trade verbiage repeated by pig racing announcers across the country, but Victor's delivery lacked enthusiasm.

Making his way up the pre-fabricated metal stands, Damon saw his mother and Charles Swickley sharing a tub of caramel corn in the middle of an aisle. Damon took a seat near the top corner where he could monitor them.

"Spy much?"

Damon looked up at Rebecca's toothy grin hovering overhead. She had a raincoat draped over one arm and was sporting muck-style rubber boots.

"I couldn't help it," Damon replied. "What's she doing with him?" Rebecca squeezed past him to the open seat on his left.

"The same thing as everyone else here," she said. "Having a good time watching pigs sprint around a muddy track." A horn sounded and six svelte swine sped off, splashing small spurts of mud, though it failed to reach the first row of spectators.

"Good thing you brought your raincoat," Damon teased.

"It might rain later. And the boots are for the petting zoo."

All six pigs turned the final corner and made their way down the stretch, with the red-shirted number three eking out a victory over the green-shirted number five.

"They weren't chasing anything," Damon observed.

"What do you mean?"

"At dog races, the dogs chase a stuffed rabbit."

"And do rabbits chase stuffed carrots?" quipped Rebecca.

"Seriously. Why are the pigs running if there's nothing in front of them?"

"Well, horses don't have anything in front of them."

"But they have jockeys. Are they trained?"

"The jockeys? I suppose."

Damon laughed and twisted skin on Rebecca's forearm. Rebecca sulked. Damon supposed she didn't want him treating her like a sister.

Victor announced the next set of racers, which looked conspicuously like the first group. Damon saw his mother look up and give him a little wave. Damon flushed and waved back. After watching the purple-shirted number one pig win by a snout, Damon and Rebecca skipped the final race in favor of the petting zoo.

Despite a lack of rain, wet straw stuck to the kids' clothing as they lay on the matted ground to get up-close views of the animals. Rebecca busied herself playing peek-a-boo with a cocksure rooster to the delight of a pair of identical twin girls decked out in matching Hello Kitty shoes and necklaces.

Movement caught Damon's eye beyond the end of the zoo. Fifty feet away, near a line of Port-a-Johns, Lirim threw his hands in the air. Skipper appeared to be pleading to him. Between the distance they stood from the petting zoo and the din of a human-animal symphony, Damon couldn't make out their words. Fifteen seconds later, Skipper stalked off toward the row of trailers shaking his head. Lirim plucked a blade of grass, popped it between his teeth and headed into a portable toilet without knocking.

Crawling into his double bed later that night, Damon pulled a sheet over his outstretched limbs, despite the heat. He turned onto his stomach and tucked his head under a flat dense pillow. A neighbor's barking dogs during his formative years had prompted this silencing maneuver and it stuck. Drifting off to sleep, Damon felt an odd sensation pass through his body. He shook his head as if rebuffing a mosquito's advances and fell into an uncomfortable sleep.

Chapter 3

Damon was momentarily dazed by the ringing telephone. He rubbed raw eyes and peered at blurry digits on the bedside clock.

"Hello?" he said groggily into the phone's mouthpiece.

"Damon? It's Gerry Sloman. What time is the fair supposed to open today?" The words rushed by.

"Gerry?" Damon mumbled. "It's seven thirty in the morning. What's going on?"

"Damon, what time does the fair open?" Gerry repeated with atypical urgency.

"Ten o'clock. Why?"

"I need you to call the county commissioner and let him know that the fair is cancelled until further notice. Then get down here to the fairgrounds. You've met a number of the Big Surf workers. I need you to give me whatever background you have on them."

"Wait, what?" Damon interrupted. The morning fog quickly lifted.

"Just make the calls and get down here. I have a dead body on your fairgrounds."

Damon froze momentarily, then quickly recovered and raced to the bathroom. He inserted contact lenses, which immediately scratched at his corneas, dressed and bounded to his Saab. Zipping through empty streets, he called the commissioner. The man let fly a litany of curses when Damon filled him in with the little he knew.

Damon then dialed Liz de la Cruz. She didn't pick up and by the time he finished leaving her a message, he was parked at the fairgrounds. The lot was empty but for a throng of police cars and a large white truck that read "Virginia Medical Examiner."

Damon jogged down the hill into the fair complex. After passing through the maze of games and rides, he saw yellow tape cordoning off the back lot where the trailers lined the woodlands. Two dozen unkempt pajama-clad carnival workers crowded the entrance of the nearby amphitheater.

"Hey you," Damon heard as he surveyed the grounds looking for Gerry.

He turned to see a top-heavy redheaded woman briskly walking toward him.

"Who are you?" she barked.

"Damon Lassard. Gerry Sloman sent for me."

"All right. I'm Lieutenant Hobbes. Gerry told me you'd be coming by. Follow me."

Gerry was standing just inside the taped barrier talking in an animated manner to two men dressed in police attire. "Gerry, I have Damon Lassard here for you," Hobbes interrupted. "The chief will be here in twenty minutes and I'm putting together a preliminary briefing for him. Once the medical examiner has taken away the body, let's start interviewing the carnival workers. And make sure incoming fairgoers are blocked from getting down here. Mr. Lassard came in pretty easily." She didn't wait for a response and walked straight to the trailer at the far end of the fairgrounds.

Gerry slapped Damon on the shoulder and followed his gaze. "That's my superior officer," he said. "And yes, that's Lirim Jovanović's trailer. He was strangled to death last night."

Gerry led Damon to the exhibition pavilion, grabbing two cups of coffee from a bespectacled patrolman carrying a cardboard tray laden with steaming Styrofoam cups.

Once inside, Gerry and Damon found a pair of folding chairs in a dark corner near the taxidermy entries. Gerry wiped his eyes with his palms. "This is a mess," he started. "We got a call at about a quarter to six this morning from Victor McElroy stating that Lirim was lying dead in his trailer. Lirim's trailer that is, not Victor's."

"What was Victor doing there at that time of the morning?" Damon asked.

"He said they start that early every morning on days the carnival is operating," Gerry said, taking a long drink. "By the time we arrived, there was a crowd of carnival workers collected outside of the trailer."

"He was strangled. Did you see him?"

"I did. He was in boxer shorts and socks lying in bed on his stomach. His head was twisted to one side so we could see red and purple mottling on his neck. I didn't see much blood so I'm pretty sure he was strangled. The medical examiner, Grace Chu, will be able to confirm."

"And the fair?"

"We'll see if the chief allows it to reopen tomorrow, but for today, the whole place is a crime scene."

"Too bad for the county, but it makes sense. Of course, here in Hollydale, there's no way you'll be able to investigate in peace. Everybody will know about it."

"I know. I assigned two officers the glamorous task of fighting off onlookers and the press until the chief is ready to make a statement. Not that he'll say much until the next of kin is notified."

"Have you spoken with his daughter, then?"

Gerry noticeably perked up. "No. We hadn't started looking for the next of kin yet. You know of a daughter?"

"Her name's Clara. She and her boyfriend are staying at the Sheraton." Damon blew over the rim of the Styrofoam cup. "Rebecca and I were having dinner at the Fish Barrel a couple of nights ago and sat at a table right next to them. Lirim and Victor came in and joined them. She and Lirim were arguing pretty loudly."

"What about?" Gerry asked, his eyes gleaming.

Damon recounted as much of the conversation as he could recall, including Clara's demand for money from her deceased mother. "You think that gives her a motive?" Damon asked, willing himself not to think of a woman as lovely as Clara strangling her own father.

"Money is always a motive. Did you get a sense that she was in a serious relationship with the boyfriend? He could be a suspect, too."

Damon recalled the touch of Clara's fingernails on his wrist and Jordan Hall's reaction. Had she just been trying to get a rise out of her boyfriend? "It looked like he was pretty serious," Damon said. "I'm not so sure about her."

Gerry gave his friend a curious look but let it pass. "All right, stay here and give me a minute. I want to tell Margaret about Clara so we can notify her and make sure she and her boyfriend don't leave town."

As Gerry stepped outside, Damon took a deep breath. If anyone he knew was a good candidate for a horrific death, Lirim would have been toward the top of the list. In the short number of days since Damon had met the man, he'd sensed tension in the air between Lirim and his business partner Jim Riley, saw him argue with his daughter, act condescendingly toward her boyfriend and have an altercation with Skipper.

Given Lirim's temperament and his attitude towards women, looking at them like a crow eyeing carrion, there must have been scores of people who disliked the man.

Damon wasn't sure he fancied being involved in a murder investigation. But was he really involved? He was just talking to Gerry about his experiences with Lirim.

Gerry returned with two French crullers and handed one to Damon. "This is stressful," he said. "A year and a half as a detective and I've never been pulled into a murder. The county only gets two or three every year."

Damon bit into a cruller.

"Tell me what you know about the others working here," Gerry said. "We both met Victor who comes off as unscrupulous. Tell me about Jim Riley."

"Small guy with a goatee and an ear infection. I sensed tension between him and Lirim, but I don't know what it was about." "Money would be my guess. I noticed that Victor and Lirim were alone doing the accounts the other day. Maybe Jim wasn't invited."

"That would be my guess, though Jim has a lackey of his own, albeit a much nicer one." Damon described Skipper and the curious comment Jim made about Skipper being his meal ticket.

"How did Skipper respond to that?"

"He didn't. And I saw Skipper and Lirim in a heated debate last night at the fair." Damon outlined what he had seen from outside of the petting zoo.

"Good. Who else do you know here?"

"Nobody. I've seen some of the other workers, but I didn't talk to any of them. Are you going to question all of the temps, too?"

"Temps?"

"College kids home on break who are working the concessions," Damon said.

"I hadn't thought of them. I'll get a list from Jim Riley and we can check them out. Of course if they just started a day or two ago, I can't imagine Lirim did something so bad so quickly that it would lead to murder."

"I guess not, though some work multiple weeks at nearby fairs."

Gerry cracked his knuckles nervously. "All these years on the force and for the first time, I think this job just got really hard."

The men left the exhibit hall. Surveying the space in front of him, Gerry spotted Margaret talking to the police chief and county commissioner and left Damon to join them.

Damon watched two lab-coated men wheel a gurney from Lirim's trailer toward the medical examiner's truck, which had been moved to just outside of the taped off area. There was a sizable body underneath a white sheet. A petite Asian-featured woman trailed the cart, presumably the medical examiner Grace Chu. As the gurney bumped along the hardened dirt toward the back of the truck, Damon noticed an assemblage of reporters and cameramen gathered among a nearby grove of fruit trees.

He instinctively looked for Bethany. Of course she wasn't there. She was a weatherperson not an investigative reporter. A myriad of news cameras laser-focused on the men loading the sheet-covered body for transport while the carefully coiffed reporters spoke with appropriate gravity impressed on their faces.

Damon drained the last of his coffee, reflexively crushed the cup in his hand, and headed over to Liz de la Cruz who stood alone watching the scene.

"Quite a morning," Damon said, forcing a smile.

"Like you wouldn't believe. And my husband is out of town for work. I had to find a neighbor to come over and pack the girls off to preschool."

"Sorry about that."

"It's not your fault. So that Lirim guy we met a few days ago was murdered?"

"Strangled. What have you heard?"

"Just the commissioner and police chief arguing about how long they need to close down the fair. The commissioner was pushing to reopen it tonight, but the chief laughed and said he'd be lucky if it they allowed it to reopen by Saturday."

"Two days will sure take a toll on the profits."

"I'm sure Jim Riley isn't pleased about that," she said. "I wonder who gets Lirim's share of the business?"

"I imagine his daughter, unless he has other kids."

"I'm sure the police will find out. Isn't there always some insurance money at stake in gruesome murders?"

"I don't know whether there's any insurance money, but you're right that strangulation is pretty gruesome. It makes it seem like there was a personal vendetta. As if someone really wanted to show Lirim how much they hated him."

The group of county employees standing near them broke up. The commissioner and police chief strode off toward the television cameras, Margaret Hobbes started toward the amphitheater and Gerry came over to Damon and Liz.

"The plan for now is to allow you to reopen on Saturday morning," he said without preface. "The carnival crew can go about the town but we're not letting any of them leave Hollydale. We'll have a twenty-four hour police presence here while we investigate. Margaret went to tell Jim Riley and the others."

"Is there anything we can do?" Liz asked.

"No," Gerry said with gratitude. "We're going to start interviewing people one by one and the chief wants you both to take off. I'll keep you up to date."

Gerry left them to join Margaret in the amphitheater where she was engaged in a discussion with Jim Riley. Damon couldn't decipher the look on Jim's face in the distance but if he had to guess, Lirim's former business partner appeared more pleased than saddened.

The sky clouded over and a moderate rain began to slick the grass. Damon and Liz quickly climbed the hill seeking the shelter of their respective cars. When they crested the rise to the parking lot, Damon saw Clara Jovanović and Jordan Hall emerging from a gray SUV trailed by a police officer who had just come out of his squad car. Clara pulled a green raincoat hood over her bowed head and moved lethargically toward them. She looked up briefly when they passed and gave Damon a piteous look that went unnoticed by Jordan.

Chapter 4

Damon took a steaming hot shower, allowing the scorching water to pound his back, then turned and challenged it to pummel his face. Stepping out, he shook with the transition from hot to cold. The sky had continued to darken and the rain picked up in intensity.

He laid in bed and called Rebecca. He could hear the industrial strength dishwasher in the background. Damon knew Rebecca's schedule by heart, and she was in between classes.

"Did you hear?" Damon asked without proffering a greeting.

"The one about the two silkworms?"

Damon cut her off. "Be serious for a minute. Did you hear about what happened this morning at the fairgrounds?"

"No," she said in earnest. "What happened?"

"Lirim Jovanović went and got himself murdered."

"Murdered," she repeated. "That guy we saw in the Fish Barrel two nights ago?"

"One and the same." He recounted his morning adventures.

Rebecca took in the story with relative ease. "I bet it was that guy Victor," she said plainly when Damon finished his account.

"Really?" Damon said. "He seemed like the only person who could stand to be around Lirim."

"Maybe, but he still gave me the creeps. He didn't say anything at the Fish Barrel. He just sat there grimacing."

"True, but he was talking yesterday when he announced the pig races."

"Yeah, like the grim reaper doing stand up."

Damon laughed. "I suppose the murderer could be Victor. But, then again, it could have been anyone."

"Clara must be on top of the list," Rebecca said. "She'll surely get the money from her mother's estate now that her father is dead. She might get Lirim's assets, too."

"They didn't appear to have been on the best terms," Damon said. "But if she doesn't have siblings, anything Lirim had will probably go to her."

They debated whether Lirim was likely to have had sired any other offspring.

"And he may have had a will," Damon suggested. "From what we heard at the Fish Barrel, it sounds like his wife had one."

"Good point. So did you hear the one about the two silkworms who had a race?" Rebecca asked, bringing their conversation full circle.

"No," Damon said flatly.

"It ended in a tie."

Damon called his mother and let her know how he had spent the morning. She engaged in uncharacteristic motherly cooing and demanded that he come over for a late lunch.

Damon feasted at Lynne's kitchen table on pastrami and Swiss and a mountain of homemade fennel slaw. During Lynne's six years living in Hollydale, no one had been murdered there. She decided it wasn't a local who had done the killing. Damon agreed. He sensed this murder was committed by someone who had a much longer history with Lirim Jovanović.

Needing a rest, Damon stretched his long legs over the end of the love seat in Lynne's front sitting room.

As soon as he laid down, his phone vibrated. He glanced at the caller identification. Bethany Krims.

Damon sat up and hesitated before answering. She greeted him warmly, which calmed him. "I saw you were down at the fairgrounds this morning," she said.

"You were there? I looked for you with the reporters and didn't see you."

"No. I saw you on film footage. I heard about the murder from one of my colleagues and came into the station early to see what was happening."

"And you saw me on tape?"

"You were talking to a woman who was putting on ChapStick while a couple of guys in long coats loaded the body into the truck."

"That was Liz de la Cruz," Damon said. "She's my counterpart over in Oakwood. Did I make it into the segment?"

"Sorry, you two were the first things cut. Did you know this Lirim person?"

"We met a few times while he was setting up the carnival. So if you know it's Lirim, the police must have released his name."

"I guess so, it was in the segment. The police must have already notified his next of kin."

"They did. I saw his daughter when I was leaving the fairgrounds this morning."

"Is that the gorgeous woman with the throaty voice? My colleague interviewed her for the segment."

"I'm sure that's her, though I didn't think her voice was that throaty."

"Maybe it sounded that way because she was competing with the rain crashing down during the interview."

"What did she say?" asked Damon.

"Nothing earth-shattering. Just the usual devastated daughter routine with a huge golf umbrella as a backdrop."

The conversation continued for a few more minutes, moving from the murder to the closing of the fair. Just before they hung up, Damon asked if he could call her "if he heard anything else about the murder." She agreed and he stored her number in his phone.

He breathed in deeply and exhaled. Bethany had never called him before.

Before returning home, Damon detoured to the nearby Safeway to pick up some staples. Traversing down the cereal aisle, he noticed Jim Riley wedging a box of granola bars into a handheld basket. Damon offered his condolences.

"Good riddance to bad rubbish," Jim replied looking up. His earlobe was pulsating and Damon couldn't help but notice several deep scratches on one of his forearms.

Damon regretted approaching the man, but he couldn't walk away now. "Still, it's horrible when anyone dies before their time," he said.

"I suppose, but he wasn't doing me any favors living. The IRS audited us last year. Lirim and Victor McElroy were skimming cash off the top of our receipts."

Damon was taken aback by Jim's frankness. "They didn't go to jail?"

"No. That's the kicker. The IRS penalized the company rather than call in their criminal investigation team. Because I own half of Big Surf I had to eat fifty percent of the penalty." He set his basket on the floor and crossed his arms. "The IRS said they were skimming about five percent, but I think it was closer to fifteen. And those two wouldn't let me anywhere near them when they were counting receipts. I was his partner, and he wouldn't even let me see the books."

"Why didn't you sue him?" Damon asked. His regret about approaching Jim had vanished.

Jim blanched. He picked up the basket and switched it from his right hand to his left and then back again. "I couldn't do that. I just couldn't."

Damon looked at him with interest. There was clearly something Jim wasn't telling him, but he didn't press the point. "At least the IRS made them stop skimming," he said in an effort to mollify Jim's agitation.

"It made them stop for a while, then about two months ago they started right back up," Jim said with venom in his voice. "He and Victor might not have been taking fifteen percent off the top this time, but it was probably almost ten. After the audit penalty, I had a better sense of how much we were really bringing in."

Jim winced and his earlobe pulsated in unison. "I should've been able to see early on what he and Victor were doing," Jim continued. "It's so obvious now. But before the investigation, it never occurred to me because the receipts had been consistent since we became partners."

Damon nodded sympathetically.

"We expect the college kids to slip the odd twenty dollar bill in their pockets, which is why we pay them so little," Jim said. "But I never expected my business partner to do it." He took a deep breath.

"Why did Lirim sell a share to you in the first place?" Damon asked.

Jim eyed Damon but didn't shy away from the question. "I think he needed the capital. He was in deep with a couple of guys who called themselves venture capitalists. Maybe venture capitalists for rednecks. I suspect that they suckered Lirim into a bad investment down in Florida. The first winter after I bought in, Lirim spent a lot of time down there. About a year later I stopped seeing the 'venture capitalists' around."

"So does that mean Clara isn't inheriting anything other than Lirim's half of Big Surf?"

"Probably not. And even though she's an only child, Lirim's half is mortgaged to the hilt. Still, I imagine she'll ask me to buy her out and I probably will."

"I suppose it also depends on whether Lirim had a will," Damon pondered out loud.

"I don't think he did. He told me his wife had one but he didn't care what happened after he was gone. He probably didn't want one drawn up because he didn't want an attorney looking too closely into his financial affairs."

The men stopped speaking as a harried father pushing a toddler in a grocery cart stopped to select a box of generic raisin bran cereal. The boy was clutching a strawberry in one hand and a flyer for the county fair in the other. He smashed the two together, leaving a bright red stain over the words "Big Surf Shows."

"I heard Lirim's wife died in an accident," Damon said after the father and son moved on.

"She did. Tabby was a really nice woman. Too nice for Lirim."

"Did she travel with you?"

"On occasion. They have a place in West Virginia outside of Morgantown. Tabby would come out once or twice every summer. She always cleaned Lirim's trailer up real nicely if you can imagine that."

"Too bad for Clara about losing her mother."

"I guess. I don't know how close they were. But the accident was tragic. Tabby got hit by a drunk driver late at night near their house. Or at least Lirim thought it was a drunk driver." He smacked his hands together. "The police found her crushed body inside a smashed up car on the side of a gravel road. None of the trees along the road was damaged, so they decided it was a hit-and-run. They never tracked down the person who hit her."

Jim turned in the aisle and selected a box of protein bars. "Sorry for unloading on you. I guess I just had to tell someone other than the police. I told Detective Sloman and the female lieutenant everything about the IRS this morning. Victor would've told them anyway. I wouldn't be surprised if he tries to pin Lirim's murder on me. But I suppose Lirim's money skimming does make me look like a suspect, especially with these scratches I got from Bertie's cat last night."

Jim answered Damon's quizzical stare. "I share a trailer with Bertie Mangrove and two others. Bertie manages one of the food stands and her cat Christof lives with us."

"Bad timing for a scratch," Damon replied.

"You're telling me. I thought the lieutenant was going to arrest me on the spot. I have to go. Now that Lirim's gone, I'm moving into his trailer once the police clear out, and I told Victor to give me all of the files from the past year. I need to get up to speed now that I can."

Damon was left standing in place, contemplating how Jim could bear to sleep in the bed of a murdered man just after he was killed.

Chapter 5

Back at home, Damon unpacked groceries, and then dialed Gerry. Jim Riley said he told Gerry his story, but he may not have provided as much information to Gerry as he revealed to Damon. Damon caught the detective just as he was about to take a dinner break after nine hours of interviewing carnival workers. Gerry accepted Damon's invitation to come over for. a quick bite.

Ten minutes later, Gerry trudged through the front door, looking significantly more worn down than he had in the morning. He passed through the kitchen, flopped down on the leather sectional in the family room and accepted the bottle of lager Damon held out.

"I hadn't thought about dinner yet, so I just put on spaghetti and popped some frozen garlic bread into the oven," Damon said.

"Sounds perfect. Thanks." Gerry took a long pull from the beer and set it on a nearby coaster. "Let me tell you, there weren't many tears shed today. I don't think a single person at Big Surf could stand Lirim."

"Including Jim Riley, I just ran into him at the Safeway," Damon said and gave Gerry a synopsis of their conversation.

"I have to admit he has a pretty good motive. Jim Riley has all of his money tied up in this carnival business, but his partner and partner's henchman are skimming. Sounds pretty damning to me, especially with those scratches on his arm." He turned to face Damon who had seated himself on the opposite end of the sectional. "I asked him why he couldn't have gone to the police, or back to the IRS after they started skimming again. He shut up really quickly. Did you get any sense of why he couldn't rat them out?"

"No. If I was him I would have hired a lawyer to go after Lirim, but when I asked, Jim became really quiet really quickly."

"I think Jim was scared of something Lirim knew," Gerry said. "It could be that Lirim was blackmailing Jim into keeping his mouth shut."

"If Lirim scratched him, could you get DNA from that scratch on Jim's arm?" Damon asked.

"I asked Margaret the same thing. She's not sure whether we have the legal right to take a swab yet and doesn't want to risk a conviction getting thrown out on a technicality. She put in a call to one of our attorneys but hasn't heard back yet. If Jim did anything, he'll have cleaned that arm until it's raw by now." Gerry scratched his own arm reflexively. "I don't suppose you saw hydrogen peroxide in his shopping cart."

"No," Damon said. "Just junk food. After being around carnival fare all day, you'd think that when he had the chance to go to the grocery store he'd buy something decent."

"Not everyone eats as healthily as you, my friend. The lab techs will check under Lirim's fingernails. If Jim's skin is under there, we'll have something."

"Is anyone other than Jim on your radar?"

"There's the daughter, of course," Gerry said and straightened up. "Even though she and Lirim were barely on speaking terms, we're pretty sure she'll inherit whatever he had. We have an officer who used to be an accountant looking into Lirim's finances. And then there's Tobin Corb. He and his wife Angela have been traveling with Big Surf for about three years, mainly working the Hall of Mirrors and Funhouse. It turns out that Lirim was fooling around with Angela right around the time his wife died. Tobin found out and a couple of the other carnival workers heard Tobin threaten Lirim at the time."

"Why didn't Corb get another job and move away with his wife?" Damon asked.

"Beats me. Maybe he wanted to stay close so he could strangle Lirim in the middle of the night."

"Good point," Damon said. "Anybody else?"

"Someone who left Big Surf about six months ago after Lirim fired him for skipping work repeatedly. He threatened Lirim on his way out of town." Gerry yawned. "We have all of the temporary workers coming in tomorrow. Not that I think there will be much there, but I'm determined to cast a wide enough net so that the fish I'm looking for is in it."

That was why Gerry had been so successful throughout his career, Damon thought as he went to the kitchen to strain the spaghetti and take the bread from the oven. He'd work tirelessly to eliminate everyone associated with Lirim Jovanović.

The men sat down to a carboholic's delight. "I wonder if Jim will fire Victor now that Lirim's gone," Damon said.

"I would if I was him," Gerry replied, swirling a forkful of spaghetti.

"That would seem to make Victor a less likely suspect. He would have to know what would happen to his job if he killed Lirim."

"True," Gerry responded, "but it still seems a little suspicious to me that Victor found the body in his bed before six in the morning."

Damon thought for a moment. "Any chance they were sleeping with each other?"

"I doubt it. Margaret pressed that point with Victor and he almost choked he laughed so hard. He could have been overcompensating, but I doubt it. We asked a number of other carnival folks whether there could be anything sexual going on between Lirim and Victor and didn't get a sense that there was."

"Maybe they met in the early hours to do their cash skimming."

"That's what we figure. Of course, when I came to the fairgrounds to get the permits signed, they were in Lirim's trailer alone with a stack of paperwork, so they may have been doing it in broad daylight. I gave a call over to the local office of the IRS and tipped them off that they should re-open their file on Victor."

Damon stabbed and twirled a mass of spaghetti. "I don't envy you, Gerry. But at least you have suspects. The opposite would be worse."

Gerry paused as if deciding whether or not to say something. He took a large bite of garlic bread and chewed slowly. Damon waited. Finally Gerry said, "Damon, I'd like to talk to you about something confidential. I can talk technical aspects of the case with Margaret Hobbes, but it's my first murder investigation and I need a set of ears to bounce something off of."

Damon nodded, urging Gerry to continue.

"Margaret has a distinct opinion on this particular issue, and while I think she's probably right, there's something nagging at me. And I can't talk to my wife about it. Trina doesn't mind me being a police officer, but she gets nervous whenever I bring up anything related to dangerous activity."

"Gerry. For God's sake, what is it?"

He drummed his fingers on the table top. "The medical examiner will know for sure after the autopsy, but Damon, there were two different sets of strangulation marks."

Damon took in the gravity of the statement. "What exactly do you mean?"

"I mean, and you can't say a word of this to anyone, it looks like Lirim was strangled twice. Dr. Chu said there was definitely a rough-edged chain used. But there are also marks that look like they were made from a smooth cord or rope."

Damon pursed his lips and blew out air. After a minute, he said, "So the killer goes in, sneaks up behind Lirim while he's asleep, puts a chain around his neck and begins choking him. Lirim wakes up and starts trashing about. Maybe he gets hold of the chain and whips it out of reach or just holds on and won't let go. But he's too weak to fight back with vigor, so the killer grabs a cord and finishes the job."

"That's what Margaret thinks happened."

"But you don't."

"Maybe," Gerry replied. "I found two things in Lirim's bedroom that could have been used. There was an electrical cord to the alarm clock and one to the bedside lamp. Forensics is taking a look at them. It's also possible that there was another device with a cord and the killer took it and tossed it somewhere."

"Either one of those sounds plausible to me," said Damon. "But you still don't believe it?"

"Margaret has worked six homicides over the past five years and it's probably what happened, but I don't have any proof so I just can't let it rest."

"How else could it have happened?" Damon asked.

"Two assailants," Gerry said quickly. "One comes in with a garrote—either a chain or cord. And if there are two people, we can forget about the second instrument coming from the trailer itself. So one person comes in and strangles Lirim. He leaves thinking that Lirim's dead, but he's not. Later, the other person comes in, armed with their weapon, and this time chokes Lirim to death."

Damon held up his fork. "Lirim would call the police after the first attempt."

"Maybe not," Gerry said. "Dr. Chu said that strangulation can lead to unconsciousness rather than death. So it's possible that the first person rendered Lirim unconscious and ran out of the trailer without checking to make sure Lirim stopped breathing. He assumed that because Lirim stopped convulsing, he was dead."

Damon picked up the thread. "Then the second person comes in and thinks he's sleeping."

"Exactly. He's lying in bed and still breathing. And it's dark so the second strangler doesn't see any marks on Lirim's neck. He does the deed and this time Lirim actually dies."

"But it would be a pretty big coincidence if two people tried to kill Lirim on the same night by the same method."

"I know. That's what I keep coming back to and why Margaret didn't want to give it a second thought after I raised it with her."

"Can Dr. Chu tell how much time went by between the first strangulation and the second?"

"I asked her the exact same thing. She should be able to tell us the approximate time of death after the autopsy. As for which ligature was used first and how much time went by between them, it depends on how the autopsy comes out. Grace had never seen anything quite like this so she wasn't sure."

"How long will the autopsy take?"

"With lab tests, probably about a week for the preliminary results."

"That seems like a long time to wait."

"It is. According to Margaret, if you don't solve a murder within the first few days while the trail is fresh, it gets exponentially harder. The chief said we need to move fast and get it done now."

Damon and Gerry were silent for a minute, eating and thinking. "It could have been like Murder on the Orient Express," Damon said.

"Is that a movie?" Gerry asked, interested.

"An Agatha Christie novel. A man gets killed on a train and it turns out he had kidnapped and killed a little girl. The dead man had twelve stab wounds, only some were right handed and others were left handed. Some were forceful blows while others just grazed the skin." Damon closed his eyes and pictured the scene in his head. "In the end it turns out that all twelve people on the train knew the family of the kidnapped girl. They worked together and each stabbed the man once."

Gerry converted the storyline into the murder at hand. "So maybe there are two killers as I suggested, but they came into Lirim's trailer together and each one takes a turn strangling him with the rope or chain of his choice." Gerry poured a glass of water from a pitcher. "So in that scenario, who do we think could be working in tandem?"

Damon thought about it. "There are two couples I can think of."

"Clara Jovanović and the boyfriend Jordan Hall are one," Gerry said cutting in. "Tobin Corb and his wife Angela would be another."

"Not the same two couples I had in mind," Damon shot back. He uncapped another beer. Unlike Gerry, he wasn't working after dinner. "I agree with Clara and Jordan. But I don't know about the woman Lirim had an affair with and her husband. Why would the wife want to murder Lirim?"

"I don't know," Gerry admitted. "But they're a couple and at least one of them has a strong motive. Who's your other couple?"

"Jim Riley and Skipper."

"You mean Spencer Boudreaux?" Gerry asked.

"I don't know his full name. Lirim and Jim just call him Skipper."

"That's Spencer. Is it the meal ticket comment Jim Riley made that makes you think he's a killer?"

"Probably not," Damon admitted. "But remember, I also saw him arguing with Lirim the night before the murder."

"True. Okay, let's say we add them to the list of suspect pairs. But a murderous duo seems far-fetched. How often do two people conspire to kill someone?" Gerry shifted in his seat. "Then again, my theory is based on two people separately trying to kill the same man on the same night by the same method."

Damon laughed. "Did you ask Skipper what he was arguing about with Lirim?"

"I did," Gerry said. "He said it was about his pay. The workers get paid every Wednesday, shortly after the prior week's fair closes. Skipper said last week he worked more hours than Victor paid him for and that's what he took up with Lirim."

"Do you believe him?"

"Honestly, I just couldn't tell. I sprang the question on him so he would have to be quick on his feet to come up with a response that sounded so reasonable."

Damon rose and cleared the table. Gerry stood up to help, but Damon waved him back down. "Relax, Gerry. You've been working your tail off all day."

"Actually, I need to head out now. We're meeting back at police headquarters soon to compare notes." Gerry thanked Damon profusely for the dinner and his insight and headed out into the soggy evening air.

Chapter 6

The next morning was the Fourth of July. Damon hadn't thought about the upcoming party at the Hollydale picnic facility in days. And he woke with the feeling that he had endured some fantastically horrid dreams during his hours of fitful sleep. Thankfully, he couldn't recall them with any specificity, though he had the sense that chains and cords played a prominent role.

As Gerry was leaving the previous night, he had told Damon the police would scour the fairgrounds for discarded implements of death once the rain subsided. If the killers had any sense, Damon thought, they would have destroyed the ligatures or at least disposed of them far away from the fairgrounds. Then again, other than Lirim, the carnival workers slept four to a trailer. A prolonged absence in the middle of the night might have been noticed. A killer could have slipped back into his or her trailer and hid the ligatures with the intent of disposing of them first thing in the morning. But by the time he woke up, if the police had already arrived, there would be no time to get rid of them.

And the carnival workers didn't have their own cars. Heavy-duty work trucks stocked with electrical supplies and huge transport tractor-trailers stood on the periphery of the grounds. The only other vehicles Big Surf brought to Arlington were the trailers.

Clara, on the other hand, could have parked on a residential street and walked to the collection of trailers. If that happened, the ligature or ligatures used would be long gone.

Gerry had informed Damon the previous evening that the last time anyone saw Lirim alive, other than the killer, was just after midnight. A half dozen of the younger traveling employees and a handful of the temporary workers set up a crude bonfire in a pit they had dug themselves about seventy feet from Lirim's trailer. They were drinking from a thirty-pack of Natural Light and horsing around. The police received numerous matching accounts of Lirim emerging from his trailer in a gray t-shirt, blue boxers and dirty socks, holding a liquor bottle in one hand and demanding that the kids shut down the party. And they did. Within fifteen minutes they put out the fire and dispersed.

Nobody else in the carnival caravan admitted to being outside after that time. So the murder occurred between twelve fifteen and five forty-five when Victor discovered Lirim's dead body. The drink in Lirim's hand could have put him into a particularly deep sleep, facilitating a strangulation with little resistance.

Damon decided to check in with Cynthia at her salon, in case anyone asked her, as the citizens association vice president, about the fair. It was early, but Cynthia's buzzed with energy. Mrs. Chenworth was holding court, with her bulk wedged into a cashmere-colored styling chair, though no stylist was attempting to tame the masses of thick brown curls swarming about the trunk of her neck. Cynthia was leaning against a Formica countertop. In contrast to Mrs. Chenworth, she looked borderline malnourished. Stringy blond hair fell flat along Cynthia's gaunt cheeks. A single patron sat in a Carolina blue pedicure chair, her toes being attended to by a fifty-year-old redhead.

Mrs. Chenworth swiveled her head at the sound of the front door's jingling bells. She stopped mid-sentence and shouted at a ridiculously high decibel level, "Damon, did you hear?"

Damon stepped inside. "I assume you mean about the murder at the fairgrounds. I came to talk to Cynthia about it in case anyone asks."

"If anyone asks?" Mrs. Chenworth countered with incredulity. "It's all anyone has been talking about. But did you hear what the police found this morning?"

Damon shot Cynthia a quizzical look. Cynthia surreptitiously pointed a finger back at Mrs. Chenworth. Damon moved an armchair from the waiting area closer to the women and refocused on Mrs. Chenworth.

Before he could speak, she blurted out, "a clothesline!" Mrs. Chenworth started rattling out loose words. "A clothesline. That's what the killer used. Did you know he was strangled? I have my sources and I knew that this Jovanović fellow was strangled. Jovanović. What nationality is that? Czech? Hungarian? It doesn't matter. Anyway, I knew he was strangled and then just this morning, they found out it was a clothesline. Can you believe it? I came straight here to tell everyone. I didn't even stop for my morning coffee."

Damon suppressed a laugh. He'd like to see how much faster a caffeinated Mrs. Chenworth could speak. He put up a hand to stop her—he knew from experience that if he waited for an opening to talk, he could be there indefinitely. It did the trick and Damon pictured her as a trained parrot that talked incessantly but halted immediately on command.

Damon asked, "Are you saying the police found a clothesline that they know killed Lirim Jovanović?" He was careful not to mention the two different ligature marks.

"Not the clothesline itself, but the clothesline that the clothesline came from."

Damon raised his eyebrows in confusion.

Mrs. Chenworth saw them, registered the query and carried on without missing a beat. "What I mean is there's a clothesline. One of those carnival workers did her laundry at the Laundromat in Oakwood, but she was too cheap to use the dryers. So she hung her wet garments between two of the carnival trailers."

Damon wondered if the woman who hung her clothes out to dry was the same person who directed him and Gerry to Lirim's trailer the day before the fair started. She had been carrying a laundry sack.

Mrs. Chenworth's voice boomed over Damon's inner thoughts, relegating them to a corner like a stern teacher. "So this woman, the cheap one, dried her laundry and took in her clothes, but left the clothesline lying on the ground! Can you believe it? Right where the murderer could pick it up!"

Damon wondered if Gerry had known about the clothesline during dinner the previous evening. Probably not. More likely, the torrential rain had prevented it from being found right away. "So did the clothesline have skin on it or something?" Damon asked. "How do the police know it's the murder weapon?"

"No, no, no," Mrs. Chenworth said in a pejorative manner. "Aren't you listening? They found the clothesline. The rest of it I mean. So there's this woman who dried her laundry on the clothesline." As she repeated the line, Damon thought the parrot analogy even more apropos. "She must have realized it was still outside and started to coil it up. Only when she gets to the end it's frayed. Well, not frayed in fact, because I heard it was nylon not rope. But it seems to her that it looks shorter than usual. So she told the police. Can you believe it? She had to tell them!"

"Okay, I get it," Damon said, finally understanding. "So the killer cut a couple of feet from the clothesline to use as a garrote and left the rest."

"I don't know what a garrote is," replied Mrs. Chenworth, "but if you mean that he used a piece of clothesline to strangle that carnival owner, then yes, that's exactly what happened. Case closed."

"Case closed?"

"Now that they know what killed him all they have to do is arrest the person who cut the cord."

"Did anyone see a person cutting the clothesline?" asked the pedicurist.

"I'm not sure, dear," admitted Mrs. Chenworth a bit sheepishly.

Damon had to hand it to Mrs. Chenworth. She might be boisterous, but she had a talent for being the recipient of a preponderance of Hollydale's gossip.

Mrs. Chenworth recovered and started a tirade about how "cold-blooded" strangulation was as a method of murder. Damon knew cold-blooded animals took on the temperature of their surroundings. He pictured Mrs. Chenworth turning a fiery red in the July heat and smiled.

Damon broke out of his reverie when he heard Mrs. Chenworth switch topics.

"That Lirim's daughter and her good-looking boyfriend went down to breakfast at the Poorboy," she said.

Damon stared at Mrs. Chenworth. "The Poorboy? Do you know when they left?"

"Of course, Damon. I gave them directions a few minutes before you arrived."

Damon shouted "thanks" and bolted for the door. He felt a strong urge to see Clara. Ever the gallant knight, he envisioned Clara looking longingly into his eyes as he uncovered rock-solid proof that placed her above police suspicion.

The Poorboy Diner was two miles from the Hollydale business strip and almost always packed for breakfast on the weekends. But on a Friday morning, it was relatively empty. Damon told the host he would be eating alone as he peered through the diner's silvery 1950s motif searching for Clara. He spotted her toward the rear of the diner. A tall black man at her table had his back to the door and another man sat facing Clara. The host steered Damon toward the breakfast bar, but Damon requested a booth in the back.

He wasn't sure how Clara would receive him, if at all. But she smiled warmly with recognition while he shed his lightweight summer jacket. He placed it in his booth and approached her nearby table.

"I'm so sorry for your loss," he said facing Clara. "It must have been a terrible shock for you."

"Thank you," she replied softly. "Even though we didn't get along very well, he was the only family I had left." Damon noticed Jordan Hall's eyes well up with empathy.

"Well," Damon stammered, unable to think of a way to extend the conversation, "enjoy your breakfast."

"Wait, Damon. Are you alone? Would you like to join us?"

Jordan frowned. The man opposite Clara shifted in his seat.

It was clear from each man's body language that he wasn't welcome, but Damon accepted anyway. Damon shook hands with Jordan who was cleanly shaven and wore a light blue t-shirt with a picture of a double helix coupled with the phrase "Unzip my Genes."

The other man rose and extended a hand toward Damon, who shook it. The man was of medium stature, in his late fifties and had one of the most unattractive haircuts Damon had ever seen. A purplish scalp stood out in front of a graying horseshoe ring, but he had managed to allow the hair at the back grow down to his shoulders. He had light olive skin and thick eyebrows rising above small green eyes. Tiny dimples highlighted his features without managing to provide an appearance of youth.

Clara introduced the man as Toma Ljubic, her mother's brother and a hard liquor distributor from Baltimore, fifty miles northeast of Hollydale.

Damon lowered himself into the table's fourth chair. "I'm sorry for your loss," Damon found himself saying to Toma after speaking the identical words to Clara only a minute earlier.

"My loss?" he replied sternly. "If you mean my asshole brother-in-law Lirim, I'm not sorry. My sister, on the other hand, is another story." Toma's eyes softened when he mentioned his sister. Damon noticed that Jordan had reached out and placed a protective hand over Clara's.

"Both, I guess," Damon replied. "Jim Riley told me about your sister, Tabby."

"And you couldn't have helped but to overhear me and my father the other night at the Fish Barrel," interjected Clara.

"I did hear a bit," admitted Damon.

Jordan chimed in, "At least now, Clara, you won't have any problems getting your fair share from your mother's estate."

"True," said Clara. "And I suppose whatever my father has is mine as well. Though that brute Victor tells me his share of the business was mortgaged beyond belief. I suspect I'll have to ask Jim Riley to buy me out."

"I spoke with Jim at the fairgrounds while you were talking to the police," Jordan said. "I asked him what he thought of buying. I hope you don't mind."

"No, that's fine," countered Clara curtly. "You know as well as I do that I have no interest in Big Surf."

"What did Jim say?" asked Toma.

"He said that after he paid off all of the loans, he could probably settle on writing Clara a check for a hundred thousand."

Clara tried in vain to suppress a smile.

"Well, between that and the hundred and fifty thousand you should be getting from Tabby's estate, you'll be sitting pretty," said Toma.

"I suppose," replied Clara who was unable to hide a look of satisfaction. "Once the police let us leave, I just want to get back to Richmond and forget all about it."

"And then maybe we can work on getting married," said Jordan.

Clara shot him a doleful look, but Jordan didn't appear to notice and began to caress her hand.

"Maybe now I can move on, too," Toma said. "I just couldn't get past Tabby's *accident* while that man was alive." Toma inflected an air of disbelief into the word "accident." He glanced at Damon and quickly changed topic to an indictment of the roadwork crews along the I-95 corridor.

Damon came away from breakfast with two distinct impressions. The first was a confirmation of his earlier suspicion that Dr. Jordan Hall was far more interested in Clara than she was in him. Only Jordan didn't appear to be privy to her thoughts. The second was that Toma held a grudge against his former brother-in-law.

Damon considered Tabby Jovanović's accident. Jim Riley said the police believed it was a hit-and-run. But Toma hinted that perhaps it hadn't been an accident after all. Could Lirim have been cold enough to cause the accident himself? It seemed far-fetched, but would explain Toma's attitude toward Lirim and provide Toma a motive to strangle his brother-in-law. Of course, if Lirim ran into his own wife's car, he risked killing himself as well.

At home, Damon left Gerry Sloman a voicemail. Damon still had a few hours before set-up began for that evening's Fourth of July party. He decided to try his hand at amateur detective work. He could use his Lexis account at the library to search newspaper databases for records of Tabby's accident.

The small cedar planked building in Hollydale was a mile and a half from the main county library and served a committed cadre of neighborhood residents. A large open second story regularly played host to local school groups and parent-and-baby reading sessions. But early Friday afternoons were quiet. Damon said a brief hello to Mrs. Stein who was staffing the front desk. He sat in front of one of the three reference computers.

Damon quickly found three hits for Tabitha Jovanović in Morgantown's *Dominion Post*. The first referenced Tabby as a volunteer at a local hospital fundraiser.

The second was an account of her accident and death. The newspaper dated back a year and a half, to December. Tabitha "Tabby" Jovanović was found deceased in an older model forest green Chevy Cavalier. The airbag had deployed, but local sheriff's deputy Jasper Horton stated that the brunt of the impact took place on the front driver's corner and Ms. Jovanović had not fastened her seat belt, effectively rendering the airbag useless. In his opinion, the collision killed her instantly. Tabby was found at 5:42 a.m. by a local man, Mr. Simon Chenter, driving along a rural wood-lined gravel road on his way to work. Mr. Chenter observed its tail end in the ditch with the car's nose pointing face forward on the road. The position was consistent with a front end hit-and-run, said Deputy Horton. Black paint was visible on the crushed Cavalier. The police were looking for a black vehicle with significant front end damage. The article was silent on the reason for Tabby's late-night excursion.

The final *Dominion Post* newspaper article on Tabby was a follow-up three days later. It provided information on an upcoming funeral, contained a brief quotation citing the deceased woman's virtues from the "widower, Lirim Jovanović," and stated that the police had no leads on the identity of the hit-and-run driver.

Damon printed out the two stories on the accident and hunted through a range of small papers looking for references to Tabby or Lirim. No other stories referenced Tabby, but Damon found an editorial in a small local paper that Lirim had written a year prior to his wife's death.

It was a sharp-tongued dismissal of an article pertaining to the storage of utility vehicles on personal property. From Lirim's response, Damon gathered that the original commentary focused on the diminishment of property value and general eyesore caused by homeowners parking commercial vehicles in their yards. Lirim admitted that he was such a homeowner and avowed that he should be entitled to do "whatever the [blank] I want" with the land he owned.

He provided his own story as an example of "the stupidity" of the author's argument. Lirim unabashedly stated that he owned a carnival business. During the winter months, he parked his trailers and equipment in an empty lot he rented at an abandoned airfield. But those same winter months provided his only opportunity for heavy repairs and maintenance. He had a "well-kept work shed with an oversized garage door" next to his home in Cheat Lake, but the larger vehicles and rides didn't fit inside. They were housed in his yard while he worked on them.

Damon visualized a run-down house and trim shed surrounded by an assemblage of hulking metal skeletons strewn over the snow-covered grass ostensibly under the repair of a bleary-eyed Lirim Jovanović.

On Damon's way home, Gerry returned his call. Damon filled him in on the details of his breakfast with Toma.

"We're the ones who asked him to come down to Arlington," Gerry said. "Margaret is interviewing him in an hour."

Damon asked him about the cut clothesline. Gerry said he hadn't learned of it until after their pasta dinner the previous evening. But Mrs. Chenworth's information wasn't wholly accurate.

The police confiscated a nylon clothesline, but it had been neatly wound inside a storage box attached to the outside of a trailer, where the carnival laundress normally kept it. Everyone who worked at the carnival or was familiar with its operations probably knew she kept it there. When the police interviewed her on the day of the murder, she hadn't thought about the clothesline. But after the rain slowed, and the police were gearing up to search the grounds in detail, it came to her mind. The police hadn't specifically told anyone that Lirim was strangled, but word passed around the carnival staff just as it had gone around the Hollydale community. The owner of the clothesline checked the storage box to see if it was still there. It was, but felt lighter. She estimated that about three feet in length had been cut.

Gerry verified that the cut was clean and likely the result of a controlled tool such as wire cutters or heavy duty kitchen scissors, rather than something crude like a knife which would have frayed the end.

Damon wondered whether he could rule out any of his internal suspects based on the fact that the clothesline had been inside of a storage box where an outsider may not have known about it. Possibly Jordan Hall. Maybe Clara, but maybe not.

Damon recounted to Gerry his library research and Gerry seemed interested. "Thanks a lot, Damon. You're really helping me out here." Damon felt like he was helping, but wasn't sure whether his "assistance" was more of a blessing or a burden to Gerry, who may have been too considerate to ask Damon to stop pestering him.

Chapter 7

When Damon arrived at the picnic facility to set up for the Fourth of July party, a small congregation of volunteers was already staking down a blue-and-white striped canopy over a large flat area. The volunteer work crew would push together folding tables under the canopy to form a large surface for pot-luck picnic food. Grills would be wheeled into place a short distance away. Damon had secured confirmation of three self-proclaimed "grill-masters," a term he considered fatuous.

Cynthia was attempting to leverage her emaciated frame to drive a stake for the canopy into the ground with a sledgehammer. Damon gently touched her on the shoulder and asked if he could assist. Cynthia acquiesced and he pounded the stake six inches deep with a pair of swift overhead blows. She thanked him in her gentle monotone voice and moved on to help string red, white and blue lights around the support beams. Damon sank two more stakes and walked over to Jackson Krims, who had been staking the other side.

Bethany's father Jackson owned a number of properties in Hollydale, including several gas stations and the Fish Barrel. His fleshy face and an ear-to-ear smile endeared him to the locals, despite his purchase of three adjoining lots to build the largest house in Hollydale.

"Has anyone gone to get the folding tables from the church?" asked Damon.

"I don't think so," replied Jackson with a smile, his cheeks red and puffing from exertion. "I brought a pick-up truck. Let's go get them."

Damon knew Jackson Krims was a kind-spirited person when it came to pleasing the Hollydale community at large, but Damon had never spoken with him about the topic presently on his mind—his daughter Bethany. As they drove the short distance to the local Presbyterian church's storage facility, Damon steadied his nerves and said, "Bethany has been doing a wonderful job on the evening weather, Mr. Krims. You must be very proud."

"You better believe it Damon," he replied. "When she first told me that she wanted to be on television I wasn't sure she had the right personality for it. But some of her natural shyness is fading away."

Jackson stopped the truck in front of the church. He turned to face Damon and asked, "So have you asked her out yet?"

Damon was taken aback. He wasn't prepared for Jackson's candor. He sputtered out a meek, "No, not yet."

"Well you better hurry up, son," Jackson responded as he exited the truck, using his hands to heft his paunch over his legs. "She just broke up with that attorney she's been with for the past few months."

"If you don't mind my asking, Mr. Krims, how did you know I wanted to ask her out?"

"Because every straight, red-blooded male who has ever seen Bethany, on television or in person, wants to ask her out. The trick is to actually do the asking." He paused to catch his breath. "I should stop. I don't want to make it seem like I think my daughter is so perfect that she'd be ideal for everyone. I know it's her appearance that initially attracts men. She looks just like my wife did thirty years ago." He walked around to

Damon's side of the truck and put a hand on his shoulder. "Damon, I like you. You have the pulse of the community and you get things done when they need to get done, but you also handle things calmly. Look at this party. You have two hundred people who plan to show up in an hour and there's no sense of panic in you. That shows inner fortitude."

Damon thanked him for the compliment. The truth was that he wasn't worried about the picnic. What he was worried about was the murder close to his backyard. Even though it wasn't his responsibility to bring a killer to justice, he felt a sense of internal accountability given his involvement as president of the citizens association and his relationship with Gerry. It was Gerry's first murder investigation and Damon wanted him to succeed.

"So do you think Bethany would say yes if I asked her on a date?" Damon asked Jackson as they loaded eight-foot polyethylene folding tables into the bed of the pick-up.

"To be honest with you, Damon, I'm not sure. She usually goes for corporate types. But I hear you've been pretty successful in your own right. So that might help. I think I know my daughter pretty well, but I can never figure out whether she'll go for a particular guy. Just ask and don't be shy about it."

After another forty-five minutes of unexacting preparations and banter with early arriving neighbors, people began to stream into the picnic area. Soon the folding tables were loaded with traditional picnic fare as well as a generous amount of ethnic fare that reflected the ever-changing landscape of Hollydale's population. An elderly couple was operating an old fashioned stand-up popcorn cart. The smell of the hot buttered kernels infused the air and competed with the aroma of hamburgers and bratwurst emanating from the grills.

A six-year-old boy brushed hard against Damon's thigh as he and two friends sprinted by. Firemen lifted toddlers into the cab of a county engine to admire the inner workings. Scores of girls shouted gleefully as they partook in a jump-roping contest.

While he was filling his plate with a heaping scoop of a pesto orzo dish, Damon spotted Bethany Krims approaching him. A spaghetti-strapped sundress hugged her figure. As they exchanged pleasant conversation, Jackson Krims' words repeated in Damon's head: "Just ask and don't be shy about it."

He was building up his courage when Bethany said, "Damon, should I be afraid?"

He looked at her closely. There was a hint of fear in her eyes. "Afraid? What are you scared of?"

She gently tugged his elbow, pulling him a step closer. "The killer," she whispered.

Damon, momentarily in a trance from the touch of Bethany's hand, didn't understand. "What do you mean, the killer?" he asked in a hushed tone.

"You know, the person who murdered Lirim Jovanović. He's still out there."

Damon was taken aback. It never occurred to him that Lirim's death could be attributable to anyone other than someone who had it in for the man personally. But with so much cash coming into the carnival, there had to be a safe in one of the trailers that was stocked with large sums. Could that have been a motive for his murder?

"I'm sure that if it was a robbery, they were only after Lirim's money and you have nothing to worry about," he said to Bethany. She led him away from the canopy to a clearing beneath a towering scarlet oak.

"I hadn't thought about robbery," said Bethany. "I was wondering if there's a serial killer running around. I know it's a little vain, but I'm on television so almost everyone around here knows who I am. There could be a psychopath out there."

Damon's mind, fueled by the exhilaration of having an intimate conversation with Bethany Krims, contemplated the thought of a mass murderer. It was too coincidental. Lirim Jovanović was a man who amassed antagonistic relationships the way others collected shot glasses. He didn't believe that happenstance led a serial killer to Hollydale less than forty-eight hours after Lirim brought his caravan into town.

Damon said as much to Bethany, and the worry lines that had dotted her brow began to fade.

"Thank you, Damon. That really makes me feel better."

Damon knew he would never have a better opportunity to ask Bethany out. They were alone, and she had sought him out for comfort. He took a deep breath. "Bethany, there's a great musical playing at the Kennedy Center downtown right now. Would you be interested in going to see the show next Friday night?"

She smiled at him, her brown eyes radiating, and his heart almost jumped through his throat. She reached out and laid a palm lightly on the biceps of his right arm. "I would," she said, then left him to say hello to her father, who was surrounded by a small group of his property managers.

Damon felt as light as air. He scanned the crowd looking for Rebecca to tell her the good news. He noticed Skipper holding a plate of cherry pie and laughing with a local girl who had graduated from the nearby high school only a year earlier. Damon approached them. Skipper greeted him genially and introduced Shawna Crane. The two met at the carnival on its opening night. With the fair on hold, Shawna said they had been inseparable for the past two days, other than during Skipper's interviews with the police.

Skipper laughed. "They've been grilling me all right. You must have told the police about the comment Jim made about me being his meal ticket because that Lieutenant Hobbes was merciless." Shawna, a fair haired waif-like girl, laughed alongside Skipper.

"I told her Jim just meant that after I have my engineering degree and some experience, we plan to go in as partners," Skipper said.

"In the roller coaster design business?" asked Damon.

"Probably. Or at least something related to carnival rides. I'll tell you the same thing I told the police. It's no secret. Jim Riley is paying for my education. I never could have afforded college on my own and I didn't want to be indebted to a bank. But Jim saw how good I was with the machines and offered to pay my way." He paused for a sip of lemonade. "After I graduate and work for a couple of years at a design firm, we plan to open up our own shop." Skipper's eyes took on the same dreamy quality Damon noticed the first time he met the young man. "I'll be doing the design work, but between the money Jim put up for college and the start-up costs, we'll be partners in it fifty-fifty. That's what he meant when he spoke with you."

It sounded legitimate to Damon, even though he wasn't sure how much money Jim could have saved if Lirim and Victor had been skimming profits from him. He thought Skipper was a good kid. He was still in his early twenties and was taking positive steps in the right direction to better his chances in life. So why would he want to commit murder? Damon mentally crossed Skipper off of his internal list of suspects.

"It sounds like you and Jim have a great plan," Damon said. As long as Jim, with his scratched arm and major motive, isn't in prison, he thought.

"I think the police do, too," Skipper said with a smirk. "After I told them about Jim putting me through school, I could sense they were just going through the motions. But they sure had a lot of information. They even knew I had been arguing with Lirim on Wednesday."

"Really?" Damon feigned ignorance.

"It was nothing. Just that Lirim was trying to cheat me out of four hours of overtime from last week's pay. You have to pay attention with Lirim and Victor—they cheat almost every one of the employees."

Damon excused the couple. Scores of people were making their way to the makeshift dance "floor" on a sizable square of grass for the disc jockey's final song before the fireworks began.

Damon saw his mother and Charles Swickley sitting across from one another at a picnic table. She was wiping the corner of his mouth with her paper napkin. Damon started to approach them but was cut off by Rebecca.

She looked particularly cute and pixie-like. Her short brown hair was fashioned with a series of barrettes, and a silky sheer skirt in various shades of mauve skimmed her knees.

"I don't think they'd appreciate you interrupting just about now," she said.

Looking for a place to watch the fireworks, Rebecca led Damon through a throng of people who had gathered into the ideal vantage points. Damon leaned forward and told Rebecca about his date with Bethany. She didn't turn around, but instead offered an ersatz "congratulations" and sped up to an opening with a view partially obstructed by a tree limb.

They watched the fireworks in relative silence. Bursts of color shattered the night sky over Washington, D.C., in time to patriotic music pumped out by oversized speakers. Damon tried to enjoy the show but couldn't. After five minutes of silence, Damon ventured a glance at Rebecca who was standing stoically beside him and staring at the fireworks. A tiny tear drop hovered at the rise of her cheek, not yet succumbing to gravity.

"Rebecca," he said lightly. "Do we need to talk?"

"No," she responded quickly, delicately inhaling to clear her nose. "I'm fine. Everything is just fine."

"Rebecca. I don't want you to be upset." And that was true. He didn't want to upset her. But he also wanted to go out with Bethany.

"Just shut up for a minute, Damon."

At least he knew now how she felt about him. It wasn't like Rebecca didn't go out with men on occasion. She just didn't let any of them stick around for long. Maybe he was the reason why.

Immediately after the fireworks ended, Rebecca made a perfunctory excuse and strode briskly past the canopy area in the direction of her house.

Damon's mother and Charles Swickley walked arm in arm toward him. She wore jeans that accentuated her still-shapely legs and a pink open-necked polo.

"Damon, what in the world did you say to Rebecca?" scolded his mother. "We just saw her run off." Lynne Lassard-Brown didn't air her frustrations often, but she was an ardent admirer of Rebecca's so he wasn't surprised by the verbal attack.

"Nothing mother," he replied.

"Well I'm sure it wasn't nothing. You better make it right with her. She's too good of a woman for you to lose, Damon."

Damon silently nodded his head. He knew she was right, but that didn't mean he was going to give up his chance with Bethany.

"Lynne and I are going to have some sherry at my place," Charles Swickley said. "Would you like to join us?"

"No thank you, Mr. Swickley," Damon responded politely. "I promised to help clean up here." While he could have handled a drink in their company, Damon didn't relish the awkward moment when he was ready to take his leave and his mother would have to decide to go with him or remain in Swickley's company.

Rebecca's reaction to his news about Bethany had dampened his spirits. As he stooped to pick up a discarded soda can, he heard Gerry's familiar voice calling his name. Damon rose and saw the detective and his wife. Trina waved and then veered toward the folding tables to make two plates of food from a smattering of leftover dishes.

"Looks like I missed the fireworks," Gerry said. While the Slomans didn't live in Hollydale, a number of county representatives usually showed their support by attending the event.

"Is the fair going to re-open tomorrow morning?" Damon asked.

"I'm not sure," Gerry said, digging his hands into his pockets. "The chief and commissioner are discussing it right now."

"Have there been any major developments today?"

"I was down near Charlottesville," he said. "Remember the couple I told you about, Tobin and Angela Corb? It turns out they both have criminal records, and his includes more than one fistfight. There was enough evidence of violence in the database to justify taking a trip down to Charlottesville where all of his arrests were made."

"Any luck?" Damon asked.

"No, other than verifying Tobin's predilection for solving his problems with physical force."

"That's a start. Have you guys ruled out Skipper yet? I saw him here tonight with a local girl. From what I know, she's a good kid, and he seems to be pretty upstanding himself."

"Unless we crack Jim Riley and he gives us something on Skipper, the kid is off of our radar."

The cell phone clipped to Gerry's belt sounded a bland monotone chime. He put it to his ear and turned away. Gerry's voice grew animated. He punched off, and turned back to Damon, his face beaming in the glow of the streetlights.

"That was Margaret," he said. "Jordan Hall just turned himself in for Lirim's murder."

Damon wasn't naïve enough to believe that physicians were above reproach or even above murder, but he hadn't seen it in Dr. Hall.

"According to Margaret, he's claiming self-defense," Gerry said. "We'll see what that means. I have to go now. I'm not sure if he's going to make a statement or hire a lawyer right away."

"You really think he'd talk without a lawyer?"

"He'll get one eventually, but on the rare occasion when a person turns himself in, we usually get a statement straight away. Of course, I've never heard of anyone turning himself in for murder."

Gerry took off in a fast walk toward his wife, spoke briefly to her, pecked her on the cheek and sprinted for his squad car, leaving her standing with full plates of food.

Chapter 8

When Damon reached home, he promptly stripped down to his boxer shorts and started doing push-ups on the hardwood floor. It was one of his preferred stress relief techniques. He switched to stomach crunches and completed several hundred before collapsing flat on his back on the sweat-covered floorboards.

His mind raced from Bethany to Rebecca to Jordan Hall and even to his mother. Since his teenage years, he had always had mixed success with the fairer sex but never had the problem facing him now. He checked himself—he didn't actually have two women desperate for his attention. Rebecca had demonstrated her feelings toward him in an unmistakable manner. But Bethany simply agreed to see a show with him at the Kennedy Center.

Damon knew Rebecca hadn't intentionally stamped out his euphoria, but Damon couldn't help but feel a modicum of resentment. He decided to wait out the situation. Rebecca was lighthearted and prone to flippant commentary, but she also had a sincere side that Damon, in an uncommon bout of optimism, believed would allow her to be happy for him.

His thoughts leapt to Clara. How would she react to Jordan's confession? Maybe she would be looking for a shoulder to cry on. Damon immediately felt guilty. The woman's boyfriend just admitted to killing her father and all he could think about was the sway of her hips.

He tore off several sheets of paper towel from a stand on the kitchen counter and mopped sweat from the foyer floor. Within minutes he was immersed in the bathtub under a thick layer of white frothy bubbles. He tipped his head back into the steaming hot water, dipping his ears below the surface.

Why had Jordan Hall killed Lirim? It was possible that Lirim's degradation of Clara had gone too far and made Jordan snap. And Jordan was African American. Had Lirim's vitriol stretched into racial epithets?

Damon wondered whether Jordan's claim to self-defense was just an excuse. How could strangling someone with a clothesline that was cut from outside of Lirim's trailer play a role in self-defense? Or for that matter, how was it possible to use two separate ligatures defensively?

One thing that did fit was the instrument used to cut the clothesline—Gerry said the murderer used an instrument that made a clean cut. Damon knew paramedics regularly used strong trauma shears to cut the clothes off of injured patients. It wouldn't have been difficult for an emergency room doctor like Jordan Hall to lay hands on a pair.

Sleep came in erratic episodes and Damon woke feeling tired. He retrieved a text Liz de la Cruz sent him late the previous night. She had spoken with the county commissioner and the fair was scheduled to reopen that morning.

Damon arrived at the fairgrounds just before ten o'clock. He wanted to ensure that the reopening went smoothly.

He took in a morning magic show at the amphitheater, then walked toward the line of silver trailers at the rear of the fairgrounds. He spotted Victor McElroy loading boxes into the trunk of a late model two-tone Chevy Caprice. Damon hadn't spoken with

Victor since Lirim's body had been discovered. He cautiously approached the stocky man.

"Victor, sorry to hear about Lirim," Damon said.

Victor hadn't noticed Damon approach and looked up. After a moment of confusion, he recognized Damon. "It sucks. And now I'm out on the street."

"Jim Riley fired you?" Damon asked, trying to hide his surprise.

"Just like that," he said with resentment. "Two days after Lirim is gone, and I'm gone, too. I never did anything but bust my ass for this company and what good does it do me? None. That's what."

Damon was amazed at Victor's vitriol, but he remained silent. Pointing out that he had been cheating Jim Riley wouldn't accomplish anything.

"What are your plans from here?" Damon asked.

"I don't know yet. The police told everyone here at the carnival not to go anywhere for a few days, but I guess that must be off the table now. Did you hear that the doctor Clara was dating turned himself in?"

"I did."

"We all heard about it this morning. That Liz woman called Jim to tell him the fair could open." He chewed the stub of a fingernail. "She told him about the doctor. Jim went around knocking on doors this morning telling everyone the good news."

"Good news?"

"That they found the murderer and it wasn't any of us. I'd call that good news."

That made sense. But Damon still couldn't wrap his head around Jordan using two separate strangulation devices. Could the medical examiner have been mistaken?

Victor interrupted Damon's thoughts. "I suppose I'll try to join on with one of the other carnival outfits.

There are more of these companies than most people think."

"Well, best of luck to you," Damon said and walked away. Victor grunted and turned back to loading the trunk of his car. Damon thought about Victor's Caprice—he didn't think there were any cars that traveled with the caravan.

At the front of the fairgrounds, Damon saw Gerry Sloman stepping hurriedly down the hill from the parking lot. "Gerry!" Damon called out.

Gerry quickly approached him. Anxiety creases lined his face, and he was wearing the same clothes he had on the previous evening.

"Celebrate too hard last night?" Damon asked with artificial optimism. Damon knew that Gerry's idea of celebrating the collar on a major case would involve a glass of wine and an early night in bed.

Gerry shook his head. "Not even close. Do you want to grab some coffee in a few minutes? At the Dunkin' Donuts? I have to tell Jim Riley to keep all of the carnival employees in town a little longer."

"Sure, I'll meet you there," Damon responded. "But you better hurry. I just saw Victor McElroy packing his bags."

The Dunkin' Donuts along the main commercial stretch of Hollydale had a façade of brick with attractive wooden shutters and a relatively small sign. It blended well with its surroundings and made a charming storefront.

The inside was modest but well-kept and had the luxury of a second floor. The upstairs bore enough space for four tables, two of which straddled a balcony overlooking the doughnut and bagel counter below.

Damon purchased a large black coffee and found an empty table on the second level. Only one other table was occupied, and the couple gathered their trash and departed just before Gerry climbed the stairs ten minutes later.

Gerry flopped down heavily in the chair opposite Damon and rubbed both eyes.

"Hold on, Gerry," Damon said. "Let me get you a hot coffee."

He returned with the largest cup they sold, a whole grain bagel and a glazed doughnut. He set the mass of nourishment in front of Gerry, then ran back down to load his hands with creamer, sweetener and cream cheese. He spilled the accoutrements on the table. Gerry grinned and said, "Do I look that bad?"

Damon gave him a big smile in return, "I've never seen you look better, man."

"I only slept for two hours last night, and that was at my desk." He looked beat.

"So at the end of a double shift, a weary policeman pulls over a car for speeding," Damon said, trying to raise Gerry's spirits. "He looks the speeder over and says, 'Your eyes look bloodshot, have you been drinking?' The man gets indignant and retorts, 'Officer, I couldn't help but notice your eyes look glazed, have you been eating doughnuts?'"

Gerry laughed. "Thanks, Damon, I needed that."

"So did Jordan give you a statement?" Damon asked.

Gerry slathered cream cheese on the bagel, took a huge bite and covered his mouth with the back of his hand. "He did. It was just the wrong one."

Damon waited for Gerry to continue. He was happy to lend Gerry an ear.

"He didn't ask us for a lawyer. Margaret and I put him in an interview room and he told us his story. It was a story all right. It sounded wrong right from the start."

"Can you tell me what he said?"

"No, but I will. I need to talk about it with someone." Gerry inhaled deeply, breathing in the sweet-smelling air that filled the doughnut shop. "Jordan said he left the hotel room at midnight after Clara was asleep and drove over to the fairgrounds. He parked in the elementary school lot and walked down to Lirim's trailer. That would have been around 12:15, which is when the bonfire was breaking up, so the timing is reasonable. Margaret asked him which trailer Lirim was in. Jordan said the one at the end."

"But he would have known that," Damon said. "When he and Clara arrived at the fairgrounds on Thursday morning, there were police all over Lirim's trailer."

"Exactly."

"So what was Jordan's reason for visiting Lirim in the middle of the night?"

"He wanted to talk about the money from Tabby's estate without Clara knowing about it."

Gerry described Jordan's account. "He said the light was still on in Lirim's trailer when he knocked. Margaret asked him what Lirim was wearing. Jordan had to think about that one. He said Lirim had on a t-shirt and sweat shorts. That was our first signal that Jordan's story was bogus. Lirim only had on boxers when we found him and when he yelled at the kids at the bonfire, he wasn't wearing sweat shorts, either. So for Jordan's story to make sense, Lirim would have put on shorts after he came out of his trailer and Jordan would have stripped off Lirim's shorts after killing him."

"Did you ask Jordan if he pulled them off?"

"No. We didn't want to break up the flow of his story. We can always ask later."

Gerry paused for a sip of coffee, looking around to make sure no one had mounted the steps to the second floor. "Jordan said he came right out and confronted Lirim about Clara's money. He thought Lirim already had it and was either spending it or hoarding it. Jordan told Lirim that he and Clara were going to get married and needed the sum for a down payment on a house. According to Jordan, Lirim became violent and started screaming at him. That seemed suspicious. No one in the neighboring trailers heard the altercation and those trailers are packed pretty close to each other."

"So they're in Lirim's trailer and Jordan's getting yelled at," Damon recapped.

"Right. And then Jordan claims Lirim stepped really close and put his face right in Jordan's. Jordan put his hands up defensively and backed away. Lirim picked up a knife from a block on the kitchen counter and started swinging it belligerently. Jordan claims he was cowering and shouting 'calm down, calm down.' And then Lirim lunged straight at his throat with the knife. Jordan dodged it, grabbed the hand wielding the blade and managed to wrench it free and onto the floor."

"Pretty dramatic."

"It gets better. Then Lirim reached for his throat and Jordan did the same in return."

"With his hands?"

"You got it. According to the good doctor, they were locked in some sort of epic struggle, each gripping the other's neck. And then Lirim just collapsed. Right there on the floor in the kitchen area. So that's not even consistent with where we found the body."

"Jordan hadn't heard that Lirim was strangled with a clothes line?"

"Apparently not. We know word went around the Hollydale gossip circles and the carnival crew when we found the ligature, but that doesn't mean Jordan heard. He's an outsider who was staying in a hotel and we made sure it didn't reach the television cameras."

"So basically Jordan Hall says he choked Lirim with his bare hands in the kitchen, while Lirim was wearing sweat shorts," Damon said.

"It's about as inaccurate as possible." Gerry squinted. The fluorescent lights shone down brightly and Gerry's weary eyes were fighting their power. "Margaret and I figure that Jordan Hall is either really stupid or really smart."

"How do you mean?"

"He may have no idea what happened to Lirim and provided a false confession. But that's helpful, because it means he's covering for someone."

"Clara," Damon said.

"That's our best guess. If Jordan knows Clara did the deed, he could be so in love with her that he decided to fall on his sword, so to speak."

"Seems a little over the top, but he appeared to be completely devoted to her, though I sensed the feeling wasn't mutual."

"So maybe he makes the ultimate sacrifice to win that devotion."

"Maybe. You said he's either really stupid or really smart. I assume that was the really stupid reason, because it points the police right to Clara. What's the smart theory?"

Gerry toyed with the gold cross dangling from his neck. "That he is the killer and he created a false story intentionally to lead us away from him."

Damon considered that for a moment. "He comes into the police station voluntarily, deliberately provides information that he knows doesn't line up with the actual murder, and the county doesn't charge him because nothing in the false confession aligns with the physical evidence."

"That's our line of thinking. I spoke with one of the prosecutors this morning. She said that unless we get

Jordan to change his story or implicate Clara, we're out of luck without something more concrete."

"What about a charge for wasting police time?"

"We can use it if we need to bring him back in later, but the county doesn't have the resources to prosecute a charge like that."

Damon finished his coffee walked down the steps for replenishments. This new wrinkle looked bad for Clara. Damon didn't think Jordan would turn himself in if he was the murderer—why draw that kind of attention. The police would now focus their efforts on Jordan and Clara. Jordan's infatuation with Clara was understandable, but otherwise, he seemed quite sensible. Could there be someone else he was shielding? When he returned, Damon asked Gerry if the police were looking into Jordan's background.

"We have been," he responded. "And we're looking even more closely now. Margaret has a theory that he has a medical malpractice claim hanging over his head and it's related. She's just not sure how."

"Did you bring Clara in for more questioning?"

"We picked her up at eight this morning, but she requested a lawyer."

"Doesn't that make her look guilty?"

"I think she's just being smart. She didn't ask for a lawyer during her first interview, but her boyfriend just came in with a confession that she may or may not know is full of holes. It makes sense for her to get protection."

"I assume Jordan is still locked up," Damon said.

"For now. We're able to hold him for a couple of days while we look into his background and interview Clara. She has a friend in Richmond who's an attorney, but he's out of town for the weekend so we put off the interview until Monday morning."

Chapter 9

Damon was sitting down to a Thai delivery dinner when his door bell rang. Clara was standing on his front porch, dressed simply in a lavender peasant blouse and jeans. Her thick dark hair was pulled back into a white butterfly clip, but a few loose strands managed to escape and fall from above her ears down the lines of her cheeks. Bare of make-up, her face's bold features were muted. Both hands were thrust into her front pockets in a pose that projected vulnerability.

Damon didn't question her presence on his doorstep and quietly invited her inside. She thanked him and followed in silence. He led her to the kitchen table.

"I just ordered Thai food," Damon said. "Are you hungry?"

"I am, thank you," she replied. The aggressive, confident manner he witnessed on their prior encounters had been replaced by a more modest one.

He opened a bottle of Shiraz and spooned out vegetable pad Thai and Rama chicken. Damon asked her how she was feeling.

"To be honest, I'm confused. But can we talk about something else for a while? I want to give my mind a break," Clara said.

So they did. Damon told her about his baseball career in Japan and the chewing gum campaign. Clara was a patient listener. In turn, she spoke about her past, primarily about her mother.

"My father was on the road most of the year, so Mom and I were close," she said. "It wasn't atypical where I grew up—a lot of the girls in town had fathers who drove semi trucks. I was an only child and Mom didn't work so we spent countless hours together after school. We'd take long walks down by Cheat Lake, which is really a reservoir."

In her loose fitting tunic and with a translucent quality to her eyes, Clara took on a mystical presence.

"Mom and Toma grew up in Romania, under the reign of Ceausescu," she said. "He was the first of the cold war Warsaw Pact leaders to open the door to western nations. But when Ceausescu's regime turned more brutal, my grandparents fled to the United States with Mom and Toma, who were in their late teens. They settled in Uniontown, Pennsylvania, which isn't far from Morgantown. It was in Uniontown where Mom met my father a few years later."

Damon listened quietly, transfixed by Clara's soft monotone voice and content to allow her to tell the story without interruption. She spoke of her grandfather, who had become a successful automobile salesman, earning enough money to buy two dealerships of his own. Before he passed away, he set up a trust fund for Clara's mother, but he never trusted Lirim, so he made the principal untouchable. The interest each year went directly to his daughter Tabby. The corpus of the trust would only become liquid when Tabby died. It wasn't a tremendous amount, but Tabby had set up a will so that Clara, Lirim and Toma split it three ways after she passed away.

"Your grandfather didn't set up a trust for your uncle Toma as well?" Damon asked.

"Mom said my grandfather was a bit of chauvinist," Clara said. "He expected Toma, unlike Mom, to support himself financially."

When Clara was thirteen, she said, her father started taking her on the carnival tour for two weeks each summer. "In those days Mom never came along," Clara explained. "Just me and my father. It was only later, maybe seven or eight years ago, that she started to join him. That was after I refused to go any more. I moved to Richmond, put myself through college and nursing school and here I am. But without Mom, of course."

Damon didn't dare to inquire into the source of the coolness between Lirim and Clara. It may have been over her inheritance, but Damon felt there was something more deep-seated that undergirded the tension.

He cleared the dishes from the table and refilled their wine glasses. Damon asked if she'd like coffee as well, but Clara declined and asked if they could move onto the leather sectional in the family room. "Damon, I want to talk to you about something serious," she said. "About me and Jordan."

"Sure," he responded. He sat down first, toward the middle of one side of the "L," giving her the opportunity to sit close to him or at a distance. She chose a space immediately next to him, and reached across his body to place her wine glass on the coffee table.

He felt the warmth and softness of her body as she brushed his thigh with the bottom of her forearm while curling back into the seat beside him. The sensual creature he first met at the Fish Barrel had returned. Clara gently placed her right hand on his knee and caressed it gently through his worn jeans.

Neither of them commented on her hand. Clara spoke softly, facing straight forward at the dormant fireplace. "You're close with Detective Sloman, aren't you Damon? That's what I gathered from everyone at the carnival."

"Gerry Sloman and I are pretty good friends."

"That's good, Damon. I don't want to wait for my lawyer on Monday to discuss what happened on the night my father was killed, but to be honest, I also don't want to talk to the police in a stale, yellow interview room. At least not the first time I tell someone what I have to say." She closed her eyes for a moment but didn't remove her hand from his knee. "I suppose I want to clear Jordan, but what I really want to clear is the air. With Jordan, with the police, with everyone, so I can move on with my life."

"Sure Clara. But wouldn't it be better if I called Gerry and maybe we could all talk about it here?"

"No Damon, please. I'd rather just tell you first. You can tell Detective Sloman everything, and I know I'll end up in that interview room, but I'd rather just get it off of my chest now. I don't really need a lawyer. I was just stalling for time because I wasn't ready to talk."

Damon nodded and placed his wine glass on the table next to Clara's.

She stopped stroking his knee, and moved her fingers up his thigh to the line of his belt. She slid her hand halfway under the upper rim of his jeans, tucking her fingertips beneath the waistband of his boxer shorts. She didn't extend her hand any further down, content to allow her fingers to rest on his flesh two inches below and to the right of his navel. Damon faced Clara, who turned from the fireplace to look at him. She smiled a silent acknowledgement of the position of her hand.

"Jordan is covering for me," she said without emotion.

"Covering for you?"

"It's not necessary, but he doesn't know that."

"He's really in love with you, isn't he?"

"Yes. And at one time, I thought I was in love with him. But I realized a couple of months ago that I'm not.

He's a wonderful man and I'm probably crazy for not feeling the same way about him as he does about me."

"You can't control how you feel, Clara," Damon said.

"That's just it. My brain tells me he's the man I should be with, that I should marry him, settle down and have a nice life. He's good looking, makes plenty of money and is very respected in Richmond. But for some reason that's just not enough for me. Or maybe the problem is it's too much for me."

"Meaning you don't think you deserve someone like him?"

"I don't know. I've batted that around in my head a thousand times. I'm not sure whether I'm screwed up psychologically or if I just have wanderlust when it comes to men."

She bent her head down to the front of his neck, just above the collarbone between his Adam's apple and shoulder and touched her mouth lightly against his unshaven skin. Clara's moist lips lingered, then parted to make an avenue for her tongue. Damon closed his eyes and breathed in deeply. The tip of her tongue made little circles as it moved delicately up and then down his throat. The palm of Clara's left hand had found its way to the right side of Damon's chest and she squeezed his pectoral lightly. With the fingernails of her other hand, still tucked beneath the waistband of his undershorts, she lightly scratched the skin just below his abdomen. Damon let out a small groan and lifted her chin so that Clara's mouth was level with his. He shifted his weight toward her and pulled her mouth to his own. He allowed their tongues to play freely with one another.

His mind told him to pull back, to stop. This woman, while beautiful and more seductive than any other he had ever kissed, was vulnerable and possibly even a murderess. Her father had just died, her boyfriend had confessed to the killing and she had just told him that the boyfriend was protecting her. And on top of everything else, he had just made a date with Bethany Krims, who he'd been fantasizing about for two years. But Clara's hands were now on both sides of his face, lightly grazing his jawline and her open mouth began a slow descent back down his neck. Damon let her continue while he wrestled with his conscience.

Clara made the decision for him. When she reached the base of his neck, she pulled back, let the point of her tongue dance playfully against his skin for a moment longer, then tucked it back inside her mouth and straightened up. She gave him another smile and reached to the table for her wine glass. Damon inched to the side so their bodies were no longer touching.

"Jordan didn't kill my father," she said. "I doubt he ever left our hotel on Wednesday night."

Damon waited for more, noticing a mosquito that was noisily exploring the joint where the wall met the ceiling.

Clara continued. "Wednesday was an early night for us. We had dinner in south Arlington with friends. I know a good number of people in this area. A few years ago, I had a nursing externship at George Washington University Hospital in downtown D.C. Most of the nurses from the program still live here. We finished dinner at about nine o'clock, then Jordan and I came back to the hotel. We haven't been talking too much for the past couple of weeks. I've been trying to find a way to break things off with Jordan but haven't had the stomach to do it. We laid side by side on the hotel bed for about an hour. I was reading a magazine and he was reviewing a medical paper on his computer."

The mosquito gained courage, and flew in a direct line toward Clara's exposed ankles. She noticed and shook a foot when the mosquito came within close proximity. It changed course and left to survey the kitchen.

"Jordan and I had discussed my mom's will a little bit. Both before and after that scene at the Fish Barrel. He said we didn't need the money, but that's not true. He doesn't need the money, but I'm not going to marry him and I do need it. I don't need it so badly that I'd murder my own father to get it, but Jordan thinks I killed him."

"Why, Clara?" asked Damon.

She closed her eyes. "Because after we went to sleep on Wednesday night, I crept out of our hotel room to meet a man. A married man I know who lives in the District."

Damon watched Clara closely. Eyes still shut, she folded her arms across her chest. It wasn't a gesture of anger but one of comforting herself.

"Jordan and I were in bed by ten thirty and he was sleeping soundly before eleven. I waited another ten minutes, then crept out of the room. I never even left the Sheraton. My companion made up an overnight work trip and booked into the same hotel where Jordan and I were staying." She opened her eyes and shook her head in a self-deprecating gesture. "I know I'm a horrible person. Trust me, I do. But it is what it is. I can't let Jordan go to prison because I cheated on him."

"Clara, you have to tell Gerry Sloman all of this." The mosquito returned and landed directly on the point of the widow's peak on Damon's forehead. He blushed with self-consciousness and shooed it away.

"I just wasn't ready to speak to the police yet," Clara said. "I feel better about it now. Maybe you could take me down to the station, if you don't mind."

"I will, Clara. You know they'll ask you who the man is."

"I know. He's an anesthesiologist at the hospital where I did my externship. He had just gotten married when I met him. We didn't do anything at the time, but the tension was always there. In the past year, we've seen each other five times. Either up here or down in Richmond. It's terrible. He has two children under the age of three and he loves them to death. He doesn't stop talking about them. I think he loves his wife, too." She wiped at dry eyes. "It's just physical with me. But I think it makes me more comfortable with the relationship we have. I know that it can't go beyond discrete encounters, so it doesn't make me claustrophobic. If that makes sense."

"It does," Damon replied.

"I hope for his sake, our interlude doesn't come out publicly. I'll stop seeing him now, and I don't want to have wrecked his marriage. I would hate for those kids to grow up without a father, or knowing that their father wasn't faithful to their mother."

Damon didn't comment. He suspected that even if Clara broke it off with the anesthesiologist, another woman would take her place. Rather, he asked, "What time did you go back to your room that night?"

"About two in the morning. I didn't want to stay away all night. I was ready to split with Jordan, but I still didn't want him knowing that I was sneaking off behind his back."

"So you think Jordan woke up while you were out of the room and he suspects you went to the fairgrounds?"

"I do. When I returned to the room, he appeared to be sleeping, but he could have been pretending. Or he could have been sleeping by then for real. But even before he made his ludicrous confession, I suspected he knew I snuck out. "

"Why's that?"

"The next morning, after the police called, we were driving to the fairgrounds and Jordan looked at me in a way I've never seen before. It was a combination of fear and protective determination. He thought I had killed my father during the overnight hours and I knew exactly what he was thinking."

"I assume the police interviewed you separately at the fairgrounds," Damon said. "You must have felt confident that Jordan wouldn't say anything about you leaving the hotel room in the middle of the night."

"I did. That's why I didn't tell the police."

"So if neither of you said anything, why did he turn himself in now?"

"I don't know. The police were digging into our histories. Some of my friends in Richmond have called me and said they spoke with the police, but I think the authorities were just grasping at straws."

Clara went to freshen her face while Damon called Gerry. He couldn't reach him so he told the receptionist at the police station to tell Gerry and Margaret Hobbes that he and Clara were coming in with information pertaining to Jordan Hall.

Chapter 10

Margaret was waiting in the station's lobby and led Clara to a witness room. She ushered Damon into a holding area and requested that he remain so they could interview him after they spoke with Clara. Gerry turned up, looking significantly healthier than he had earlier in the day. He nodded at Damon as he passed by on his way to join Margaret and Clara.

Damon surveyed his surroundings. It reminded him of a dentist's office, except not a single picture hung from the once brash, but now muted, pink and green flowered walls. Old magazines were strewn about a low center table.

Damon sat in an uncomfortable chair and read an article in *Smithsonian Magazine* about Samoa's decision to move across the international date line to the west. The government of the tiny South Pacific nation had passed a law to align the country's date with nearby Australia because it was difficult to accomplish business with the Aussies on Mondays when the Samoans were still enjoying their weekend. The upshot was that December 30, 2011, was never recognized by the Samoans—when the clock struck midnight after the night of December 29, the next minute was twelve o' one on December 31.

Damon's thoughts turned to Gerry. He probably felt similar to the Samoans who lost a day. Gerry had seen a murder confession vanish.

Damon felt a chill of sweat as the thought crossed his mind that Clara and Jordan had concocted an elaborate ruse to allow the pair to murder Lirim. It would account for the two separate ligature marks. But that didn't add up. The police would question the anesthesiologist and he would confirm Clara's story. And that in turn would clear Clara, unless the anesthesiologist and Clara were the co-murderers. Damon didn't relish the thought of a new suspect.

Damon's cogitation was cut off when Gerry stuck his head through the door. "Are you ready?"

Damon looked up. Despite the lateness of the hour, which was approaching eleven o'clock, Gerry was clean shaven and wearing a crisp white dress shirt and blue blazer. Damon followed him into an interview room, which Gerry described as the one for "friendly" witnesses. It was a square box of ten by ten feet, with light orange painted walls and a small window overlooking a massive parking lot. Margaret joined Gerry and Damon around an oblong table and brought in a bottle of water for each of them.

They took Damon methodically through the conversation he had that evening with Clara. Damon left out the three-minute interval of interwoven tongues and mashed bodies but relayed the remainder with as much accuracy as he could muster. From the look Gerry gave him when he recounted their move from the kitchen table to the leather sectional, Damon gathered that Clara hadn't shied away from that part of the story.

After forty-five minutes, Gerry walked Damon outside to his car.

"I drove Clara here," Damon said when they reached the Saab. "She took a taxi to my place."

"I know. One of the patrol officers gave her a lift back to the Sheraton."

"You're not keeping her here?" Damon dug around in his jeans pocket for his keys.

"No. I had a brief conversation with the anesthesiologist before we brought you to the interview room. He volunteered to come into the station tomorrow morning."

Damon lingered at the car door. "Will Clara and Jordan both be off the hook once you speak with him?"

Gerry gave him a knowing smile. "Would that suit you?" he asked with friendly maliciousness.

"Let's not go there," Damon responded. "But she told you?"

"She did. No worries, I won't say anything. Especially when Friday night with Bethany is quickly approaching." Damon had told Gerry, with pride, that very morning at the Dunkin' Donuts about his upcoming date. Gerry switched gears back to the case. "It doesn't let either completely off of the hook, but once we confirm the story, we'll have to tell Jordan where Clara was the night Lirim died. I suspect he'll recant his confession on the spot. Theoretically he could have had the time to get to the fairgrounds and back while Clara was with the other doctor. But it seems pretty unlikely, so he'll drop to the bottom of the suspect list."

"Will you ask the anesthesiologist's wife if he was home on the night of the murder?"

"Probably not. The guy might be a slimeball, but we try to avoid wrecking families when we can avoid it. We'll confirm with the Sheraton that he booked a room on the night in question. The problem is, even if he was staying at the hotel, it doesn't help us much. He could have gone on a late-night murder outing with Clara or he could have watched television in the hotel room to provide Clara an alibi while she killed her father."

Damon drove home through the intensely lit streets. The sidewalks were crammed with people. Saturday night revelers crowded rooftop bars and upscale clubs on the busy streets surrounding Arlington's police headquarters. But two miles away, when Damon entered the pocket of Hollydale, the crowded sidewalks gave way to empty ones, save for a smattering of late-night dog walkers.

He had a message from Rebecca, apologizing for her emotions from the previous night and asking Damon to call her back. He looked at the clock. Twelve fifteen. Rebecca might still be awake but he wanted to speak to her in person. He sent a text message asking her to meet him at his house for coffee in the morning.

After taking out his contact lenses and scrubbing his face with a citrus-smelling soap that had appeared in his bathroom after one of his mother's visits, Damon climbed on top of his bed's comforter. He remonstrated himself for giving in to temptation with Clara earlier that evening. He had longed to take out Bethany Krims for two years, and six days before that dream became a reality he was exchanging saliva with a woman he just met. He wondered whether he would have had the fortitude to halt the encounter had Clara not done it first.

Had Clara really been too timid to go directly to the police? Damon didn't have too difficult of a time landing dates, but Clara was a breathtaking woman. And she had thrown herself at him. He thought hard and put his ego in check. Clara knew he was close to Gerry Sloman. Was she trying to curry favor with Damon so that he would defend her to the police?

Damon checked his phone, saw Rebecca's confirmation of "ok, be there at nine" and then opened his laptop. Margaret and Gerry didn't know that Clara hadn't told Damon the name of the anesthesiologist and the detectives used it freely. Dr. Anthony Weams. Damon didn't have access to the library's Lexis account remotely, so he decided to see what he could find using the Internet.

A straight Google search followed by a LinkedIn profile using George Washington University Hospital as a key word revealed a basic biography of the man. College at Washington University in St. Louis, medical school at Penn, followed by a residency at George Washington, where he was now on staff. Damon found a few distinctions and awards but nothing more. What had he expected to find, a detailed account of a crime spree?

He went to Facebook and waded through a bevy of profiles for men named Anthony Weams until he found the right one. There material available was sparse, but he found a tidbit of new information. Dr. Weams had attended "Battle Park High School." Damon plugged the school's name into his search engine and inhaled sharply when he saw the result. The high school was located less than ten miles outside of Uniontown, PA, where Clara's grandparents had settled and only fifteen miles from the Cheat Lake suburb of Morgantown where Clara had grown up.

Based on his year of high school graduation, Damon calculated Anthony Weams to be thirty-five or thirty-six. Probably seven or eight years older than Clara. Damon couldn't find any information about Clara online.

He typed in "Tony" Weams rather than Anthony Weams and coupled it with Battle Park High School. Several local newspaper stories appeared from archived sources. Every one centered around Tony Weams' accomplishments on the baseball diamond. He was a starting second baseman in his junior and senior seasons, managing an all-conference nod in the latter. It gave Damon an idea.

He could take a road trip to the Uniontown-Morgantown area after making sure the fair closed down smoothly the following day. It was only a three-and-a-half-hour trip. If he had to stay overnight, Mrs. Stein would be perfectly happy to fill in for him at the library on Monday morning.

Maybe Tony Weams' baseball coach would remember something about Anthony and Clara. Given the seven or eight year age difference, the chance of a history between two back then was remote. Unless Anthony had a younger sister who was the same age as Clara. Maybe they knew each other in their youth, even if they didn't start having a physical relationship until years later and two hundred miles away.

Damon shook his head. He wasn't a police officer or even a private investigator. He could ask Gerry to go, but the detective was busy and Damon didn't want Gerry to forbid Damon from making the journey. Instead, Damon sent Gerry an e-mail providing him with the information he found about the proximity of Anthony Weams' high school to Clara's hometown. Gerry and Margaret could use it the following morning when they interviewed Weams. Damon wouldn't make a decision about a trip until after he asked Gerry whether Weams divulged a former relationship with Clara.

The next morning Damon woke refreshed. After a run along one of the many paved trails that wound through the county, Damon put on a pot of hazelnut coffee, which he knew was Rebecca's favorite. He prepared apple cinnamon pancakes and sliced a fresh mango and strawberries into a clear glass bowl.

When she arrived, Rebecca appeared not only to have recovered from two nights earlier but was more assertive than usual. She may have been overcompensating, but everyone had to manage their emotions. Rebecca strode into the kitchen as if she hadn't let tears betray her feelings for Damon. She had replicated her pixie look from the Fourth of July party, with an array of barrettes and a short gauzy skirt. Damon thought the look suited her well and told her so.

"Thanks, I needed to liven up my look," she said.

He filled a mug with coffee, found a pair of natural sugar packets in an overhead cabinet, and handed the offering to Rebecca. She sat at the table with both feet tucked in under her backside.

"The pancakes look great," she said.

"Thanks. Listen, Rebecca, I'm glad you came over."

She interrupted him. "Damon, Friday night was ridiculous. It was immature of me not to be completely happy for you. I want you to be content and if dating Bethany Krims accomplishes that, I'm all for it."

"Rebecca, you don't have to say that."

"But I do, because it's how I feel. So can we just put it past us and move on? You can even tell me about next Friday night after the fact. But only if you want to, of course."

"Thanks, Rebecca. You really are my best friend, you know."

"I know, friends without benefits." She sighed dramatically. "Except these ridiculously good pancakes."

While they ate, she asked whether he had spoken any further with Gerry about the murder. Damon gave her as much background as he could without supplying details privy only to the police and himself. He did tell her about Clara's admission to him the previous night and his evening at police headquarters. Rebecca gave him a questioning look when he divulged that Clara had come to his house but she didn't press it.

The fair was more packed than Damon had anticipated for a Sunday morning. Between the two-day closure and the fact that it was a weekend, people had foregone their standard Sunday routine to ensure a few final hours of wholesome outdoor entertainment. Damon caught up with several Hollydale residents and bought himself a funnel cake loaded with powdered sugar. He saw Skipper holding hands with Shawna Crane near the "Strongman Striker" game and gave them a wave from a distance. Upon reaching the back of the grounds, he spotted Jim Riley. Jim waved him over.

Damon asked whether the police were planning to allow his crew to leave after the Arlington fair ended that afternoon.

"They are. We'll all be in Manassas, which is pretty close by. And they interviewed a number of people again yesterday, so they're letting us go, as long as everyone stays with the carnival."

"What about Victor?" Damon asked.

"I asked Lieutenant Hobbes the same thing. She said that after today he was free to go home but that he couldn't leave the general area for a while without getting their permission."

"He lives nearby?"

"I think his place is near Front Royal, a good bit west of here and up by the Virginia-Maryland border."

Damon agreed with the police's decision. They couldn't keep a traveling operation grounded indefinitely without concrete evidence. And their travel was local, so it's not as if the police wouldn't know where to find the workers.

"Do you have any big changes planned for the carnival now that you're running things solo?" Damon asked.

"Technically it's not all mine yet, but Clara told me I could run things as I see fit until we figure out a final price for her share and get all of the paperwork done. I'll make some internal structural changes, but nothing that will impact the public's enjoyment. The toughest part will be figuring out new storage space for this winter. Lirim had a place near Morgantown where he kept all of the equipment."

"I thought Skipper did the repair work," Damon said, even though he recalled Lirim's newspaper editorial.

"Small patchwork fixes, yes. But not the major repairs. He could do them sure enough, but it takes too long and we don't want anything out of commission during the spring and summer months while the fairs are running."

Damon's phone vibrated just as he returned home. It was Gerry.

"What's the good word?" Damon asked, getting out of the car.

"I wanted to thank you for the information you sent last night on Anthony Weams, even though it didn't lead anywhere. When we interviewed him this morning, Dr. Weams said he didn't know Clara when he lived in western Pennsylvania. He said he hadn't even known she came from that part of the country."

"Did his story match up with Clara's?"

"To a tee, unfortunately. And the hotel's reservations desk confirmed that he booked a room in his name on the night in question."

"So Jordan Hall's off the hook."

"For now. When Margaret told Jordan what Clara had done, he immediately retracted his confession. We're still going to keep our eye on him and Margaret made him sweat a little by talking up a possible obstruction of justice charge. But we won't press it unless we find new evidence linking him to the murder."

"I almost feel bad for the guy," Damon said. "Too much love for someone who doesn't love you back." He thought of Rebecca.

"Margaret said he was almost in tears when she told him about Clara and her late-night tryst."

"Better to find out sooner than later. Where does that leave your investigation?"

"Pretty close to square one. Margaret wants me to focus my efforts for now on Tobin and Angela Corb. She's the one Lirim slept with and they both have criminal pasts. To be honest, I'm not sure if it's the right place to look, but I'm letting Margaret take the lead. She has the murder investigation experience and it's not like I have anything better to push."

Damon stood in the entryway to his home, debating whether to put together an overnight bag for a drive to Uniontown or to just leave well enough alone and entrust the matter to Gerry and the other professionals. He closed his eyes, breathed in deeply, and decided to take the trip.

There was something inside him that wouldn't allow his mind to be at peace until he had done all he could to find out who killed Lirim. More than anything, he found it exciting. Life had its thrilling individual moments, but only rarely did a person participate in an endeavor that was suspenseful for days on end.

Chapter 11

Traffic was light on a Sunday in the summer going west toward the Appalachian Mountains. Damon put down all four windows and opened the sunroof—the breeze felt good against his face. He thought about who he should approach. To start, he decided on Anthony Weams' baseball coach and Lirim and Tabby's neighbors.

The difficulty was figuring out how to present himself. He didn't dare pretend to be a police investigator. He could pose as the son of one of Lirim's childhood friends who was passing through the area. Then again, given Lirim's surly disposition, even the child of one of Lirim's friends might not be welcome. Designating himself as a friend of Clara's would probably better serve his needs.

It wasn't until he reached Uniontown in the late afternoon that Damon realized he had failed to look up the baseball coach's name or address. School was out on summer break, so going there wouldn't help. Not to mention that the coach now probably wasn't the same person who was managing the team when Anthony Weams was chasing fastballs eighteen to twenty years earlier. He castigated himself for the lack of forethought.

The information he could glean about Battle Park High School from his phone didn't include anything on the current baseball coach. Damon didn't have a model that displayed full web sites, just those with dedicated mobile pages. He thought about calling Rebecca and asking her for help, but decided to keep his trip secret for now. If his search turned up empty, no one needed to know how obsessed he had become with the murder of Lirim Jovanović.

Damon steered his car through the downtown streets in search of a friendly place where he could gather information. He stopped at a diner on a busy street half a mile from the Uniontown mall. A short line of people smoking dotted the sidewalk to the left of the entrance. The interior of the restaurant was so brightly lit Damon had to narrow his eyes upon entering. Sitting at the breakfast bar, he ordered a lemonade and asked the waitress if she knew the baseball coach at Battle Park High School. She responded politely that the school was "a ways out of town" and she didn't know any of the coaches. But when she returned with his drink, she brought one of the hostesses and introduced her as a rising high school senior.

"You're looking for the baseball coach at Battle Park?" the girl asked, knotting shoulder-length kinked black hair with her index finger. Acne and light freckles were blanketed by heavy pancake make-up, usually reserved for women three times her age.

"I am," Damon replied. "Do you go there?"

"No, but I have friends who do. I can find out in about ten seconds." Which she did. The hostess reached into the front pocket of her apron and removed a smart phone. She pressed a speed dial code, spoke quickly and gave him a thumbs-up in ten seconds flat. But she kept talking for another five minutes, and, without failing to remove the phone from her ear, seated a young family who had just approached the hostess stand. Damon sipped his lemonade patiently. It was terrible—made from straight powder and without enough sugar. But by the time he choked down half of it, the teen returned and gave him the name of David

Johnson, who taught biology when he wasn't coaching the team.

Great, Damon thought sarcastically, could there be a more common name? The phone book could be littered with David Johnsons and D. Johnsons. And he didn't even know whether this particular one lived in Uniontown.

But the hostess had even more information for him—a diamond in the diner. She didn't know whether the coach would be there, but there was a baseball complex five miles northwest of town that hosted high school summer league games almost every Sunday night during June and July.

Damon wrote down directions to the park and slipped the hostess a twenty dollar bill but left the remainder of the lemonade on the counter.

At six-thirty in the evening, the mid-summer sun had not even started to set. The Fred Williams Memorial Baseball Complex was impressive. It boasted four diamonds, each stretching out from a central area that was occupied by a modern locker room facility in the shape of an octagon. The result was visually stunning. Four fields combined to form a giant square, or diamond, depending on the vantage point. The triangular-shaped gaps that formed between the edges of each pair of fields were filled by flat seated bleachers that could be used by spectators to watch either side— the first base line of one game or the third base line of another.

And true to the hostess's word, the complex was brimming with high schoolers. Damon climbed to the apex of the closest set of bleachers and peered down around him. Games were in progress on three of the diamonds and on the fourth, players were stretching out and preparing to commence play. The scene warmed him. Here, in the heart of the country, the nation's pastime was being played with gritty determination in the faces of the young players.

He stepped down the bleachers toward a game that was in the middle of the third inning. The scoreboard didn't denote team names, just "Home" and "Away" so Damon couldn't immediately establish whether the teams were local. He located a couple who looked to be in their mid-forties sharing a large cardboard tub of popcorn. They were probably the parents of one of the players and good candidates to know the local coaches if their son's team was from the area.

Damon sat down beside them and asked if they knew of David Johnson who coached the local Battle Park high school team.

"Sure do," the man replied, wiping a smear of butter from his upper lip with the back of his hand. "My son, he's in the bullpen out near left field, is on the junior varsity team at Battle Park. He's trying out for Coach Johnson this fall. The kid has a great arm, but still has some control issues we need to get in order." He pointed toward the bullpen where six or seven youths sat bowlegged having what appeared to be a spitting contest.

"I pitched in school, too," Damon said casually, without detailing his post high school career.

They discussed the merits of a few recent changes in pitching styles, then Damon asked whether he knew if Coach Johnson was at the complex that evening.

"Not tonight," responded the man, chewing through another handful of kernels. His wife looked on, horrified at the sight of him eating with his mouth open while speaking. "I happen to know that he's on vacation this week. A group of former hurlers, including Coach Johnson, run summer pitching camps and our son is in one of them. But my boy told me the coach left this weekend to take his family up to Cape Cod."

"You wouldn't happen to know if he coached the Battle Park team fifteen to twenty years ago would you?"

The man laughed heartily, then coughed as the skin of a popcorn kernel caught in his throat. He made a series of hacking gestures, chewed what had apparently come back up into his mouth and re-swallowed. His wife, now completely mortified, turned to face the opposite direction, pretending to be enamored with the game even though her son remained in the dugout.

"It definitely wasn't Dave Johnson, that's for sure. He's closer to your age than mine. The coach back then was Randy Wadecraft. Randy was there as long as I can remember. Son of a bitch cut me after my sophomore year. Granted, I couldn't see a change-up coming to save my life. But I played a mean third base."

"Do you have any idea where I might find him?" Damon asked.

"That's easy," he said with vivacity. "He should be right here at the complex. His grandson catches for a team from just south of Pittsburgh and they're playing tonight. Randy never misses a game."

He turned to the woman beside him. "Hon, do you need another soda? I'm going see if I can locate Randy Wadecraft for this gentleman and can get a Diet Pepsi while I'm down there."

She nodded her head and gave Damon a sugary smile.

The man, who by then had introduced himself as Charles—"but everyone calls me Ducky"—Traduck, led Damon down to the concourse. Walking quickly for a man of considerable girth, Ducky soon spotted the green and gold jerseys belonging to the team from outside of Pittsburgh. He approached the edge of the field, first searching the field and pointing out Wadecraft's grandson crouched behind home plate. He turned his attention to the bleachers, scanned for a few seconds and spotted his prey. "Randy Wadecraft," he said to Damon. "Fourth row up, a few feet in from first base. Old guy sitting by himself with the shaggy gray hair and jean vest."

Damon thanked Ducky with a firm handshake before Mr. Traduck set off for the concession stand.

As Damon made his way over to the former high school coach, the pitcher flung a wild ball into the dirt. It skipped past Wadecraft's grandson to the backstop. The boy flipped up his mask, and sprinted after the ball. A runner on first base used the opportunity to take second, then dug in his heels and raced for third. The catcher saw the move, picked up the baseball and whipped a bullet straight and low into the outstretched mitt of the third baseman, who tagged the runner out before he could complete his feet-first slide into the base. Each Wadecraft, the elder in the stands and the younger trotting to the dugout, pumped a fist in the air.

"Heck of an arm on that catcher," Damon said with enthusiasm taking a seat one step down from Randy Wadecraft.

"You better believe it," he replied with pride. "That's my grandson."

Damon admitted he knew the two were related because Ducky Traduck had pointed out the pair of them.

"Charles Traduck," Wadecraft said. "I remember him. He couldn't hit worth a lick thirty years ago. I think he still resents me for cutting him. No wonder he didn't come over to say hello."

"Have you seen his son pitch?" Damon asked, hoping to establish a rapport with the elder coach.

"Sure, a few times," he said crinkling his eyes, which accentuated the ceases in his brow. "He has a pretty good fastball for a kid his age, but his accuracy needs work."

"That's what Ducky said."

Randy laughed. "So I hope you're a college scout looking at Damon," he said.

"Damon?"

"My grandson who just cut down that runner at third."

"You confused me. My name's Damon as well. Damon Lassard." They shook hands. "And no, I'm not a scout."

"Too bad," he replied, crinkling his eyes again, which Damon now recognized as a mouthless smile.

Damon recounted his own baseball history, this time not leaving out the parts about college and the Japanese leagues.

"Pretty impressive, son," Randy said when Damon finished his story.

They stopped conversing to watch Damon Wadecraft stride to home plate for his turn at bat. He was a strapping young man wearing a jersey shirt a size too small, which accentuated his chest and arm muscles. Damon wondered whether there was a particular high schooler he was trying to impress or if his mother had just washed the uniform too many times. After taking two pitches for balls, Damon Wadecraft tore into a fastball and sent the ball skyrocketing toward center field. It landed in the center fielder's glove, only feet from being a home run. But the team's runner on third base easily tagged home.

"Solid sacrifice," Damon said to shore up the good graces he had established with Randy. "No doubt about getting the runner home with that hit."

"Every RBI helps pad the stat sheets," Randy replied and then turned to face Damon squarely. "But you didn't come over here to talk about my grandson, did you?"

Damon blanched, but raised his courage and supplied Randy with an abbreviated history of his current position, the murder at the fair and finally, Anthony Weams. Damon said Anthony had been brought into the investigation because of his relationship with the murdered man's daughter who grew up in a suburb of nearby Morgantown. He didn't detail the scandalous nature of the relationship between Anthony and Clara.

Randy Wadecraft took the account in stride and didn't ask why Damon rather than a police officer was sitting next to him.

"Tony Weams was a good kid and a pretty good infielder," he said. "Smart, too. He didn't take the dummy classes like some of the players."

"Do you remember a girl named Clara Jovanović hanging around with him?"

Randy considered the question thoughtfully. "I can't say that I do," he said and used the back of his hand to flip unkempt gray hair from the back of his neck.

"I'm not surprised. She's probably seven or eight years younger than Tony, and I can't imagine a high school ball player knowing someone that young, unless she was a friend of the family or the sister of a buddy."

"I agree with you there," Wadecraft said. "It's a long time ago so I don't remember everything, but I don't specifically recall Tony having any friends outside of Battle Park. And I'm pretty sure he had a girlfriend at the school, too."

Suddenly the coach's wrinkled eyes began to gleam. Specks of blue shined out from behind gray irises.

"What's that surname again?" he asked sharply turning to face Damon.

"Jovanović. Clara Jovanović. The father who was killed was named Lirim. The mother was Tabby or Tabitha."

He tapped his forefinger against the wrist of his opposite hand. "Son, there's something there all right, but it has nothing to do with Tony Weams, at least I don't think it does."

Damon raised his eyebrows, urging Randy to proceed.

"Lirim Jovanović. I never met the man, but I remember where I heard the name. Maybe fifteen or sixteen years ago or so, there was a rumor floating around the school. In the teaching and coaching circles that is. It was about a guy from Morgantown who was peddling photographs of little girls. The naked kind."

Damon's jaw didn't drop, but his mouth reflexively opened.

"Word was going around in case anyone saw someone approach one of our students. Though I don't think he was interested in high school girls. More like ten- or eleven-year-olds was the story. Anyway, I heard he had a few dozen pictures and he was in some sort of business where he traveled a lot and sold them on the road. At the time, I figured he was a trucker, but I suppose a carnival owner would work just as well."

"And you think it was Lirim Jovanović?" Damon asked.

"I do. I remember somebody saying the Morgantown sheriff was looking into it. After a week or two of talk at the school, we didn't hear about it again."

"How did the school come to hear about it in the first place? Did Lirim approach one of the teachers trying to sell the photos?"

"I couldn't tell you, Damon. I just don't know. You should try the sheriff's office down in Morgantown. They might have a record of it."

Damon knew that would be his next stop. He thanked Randy and waited in line at the concession stand for a foot long kosher hot dog that he doused with thick orange cheese from an oversized squeeze bottle.

He ate in the front seat of his car, mopping cheese from the corners of his mouth with a tissue, and considered the ramifications of Lirim Jovanović as a small-time child pornography distributor. At least Damon assumed he was small-time.

Had word trickled down at Battle Park from the teachers and coaches to the students? To Anthony Weams? No, assuming the coach had his timeline correct, Anthony would have been in college by then.

Was Lirim taking pictures of his own daughter? It would account for Clara's animosity toward him. She would have been thirteen or fourteen at that time. Older than the ten or eleven cited by Randy Wadecraft, but Randy had only heard rumors. And what was to say that Lirim hadn't been in that line of business for years by the time word spread to Battle Park from Morgantown?

Damon considered the impact of the information on Lirim's murder. The killer could be totally unrelated to Big Surf—a former victim who decided to seek her revenge. Or after going through years of therapy, a victim recounted her tragic childhood secrets to her current husband or her father who hunted down Lirim Jovanović and choked the last breath out of him.

Chapter 12

The sun was inching down toward the horizon when Damon left the baseball complex. He drove south toward Morgantown. The West Virginia University emblem emblazoned everything from street banners to bumper stickers. He found a Hampton Inn and registered for a single night.

Using a public computer on the first floor of the hotel, Damon conducted basic searches using Lirim's name and different terminology that could relate to child pornography. No positive results turned up, and more than half of the sites that his searches found were blocked by the hotel's computer security system. He wrote down directions to the sheriff's station in town and to the Jovanović home, using the address he located by a search of the county's electronic property tax database.

He debated dialing Gerry but decided to wait until after he had spoken with the sheriff in case he learned something useful. Not that he was sure a sheriff would speak about a potential criminal matter with someone outside of the law enforcement profession.

After breakfast the following morning, Damon easily found the Monongalia County sheriff's station, a squat unremarkable structure on a side street. Damon entered an empty lobby. It was small and furnished with a pair of brown stuffed armchairs and a worn navy blue sofa. Framed portraits of mayors, city council members and the sheriff hung above brass name placards.

Damon considered Sheriff Ravi Anbani's photograph and wondered how many people of Indian descent resided in Morgantown. His contemplation was interrupted by a gruff "Can I help you?" coming from the direction of an interior aperture at the back of the lobby. Through it, Damon saw a thin hatchet faced woman smacking gum inside her red lipsticked mouth.

Damon tried to disarm her with charm, but she had been fending off ordinary citizens, whether well-intentioned or not, for too many years to be taken in. As she repeated for a third time that it was simply not possible for Damon to see the sheriff if he didn't have an actual crime to report, the front door opened and Ravi Anbani strode in wearing casual dress. He looked ten years younger in person than in his portrait. His face was thinner and he had a wiry build that was not visible in the picture.

The sheriff's demeanor was the antithesis of the desk clerk's character.

"Good morning," he said to the receptionist with a wave. "Good morning sir," he said in Damon's direction. "Is Carla taking care of you all right?"

Carla interjected before Damon could speak. "He wants to talk to you, Sheriff, but he's not a county citizen and he doesn't have a crime to report."

Anbani looked closely at Damon, but with bemusement. Damon suspected that the sheriff and receptionist didn't always see eye-to-eye on matters of protocol. "Where do you hail from, young man?" he asked with artificial gruffness which belied his deportment.

Damon played along. "Arlington, Virginia, just outside of Washington, D.C."

"That's an awfully long ways away," mused the sheriff. "I think I can spare a few minutes to find out why you came to see me."

He led Damon through the door, past Carla who began to peck determinatively at her keyboard, and into his modest office. He went to retrieve mugs of police-house coffee from down the hall.

Moments later, the sheriff handed Damon a cup of java and sat behind a desk that was too large for the room.

"Sorry the coffee looks like mud," Anbani said. He waited a beat and said with a chuckle, "It was ground just a minute ago."

Damon laughed.

"So, now that you've made it past my crack security team," the sheriff said, "what can I do for you?"

Damon regaled him with the events of the past week, including what he had passed along to Gerry. He left out any suggestion of the information funneled in the other direction. Just because the sheriff may have broken nonsensical protocol in speaking to him, that didn't mean he would condone a detective sharing case information with a private citizen.

Finally, Damon came to the bombshell unloaded on him by Randy Wadecraft the night before. "Randy said that about fifteen years ago, there were rumors going around Battle Park High School up near Uniontown that Lirim Jovanović was taking pictures of pre-teen girls and selling them."

The sheriff had waited patiently and impassively throughout Damon's account. He now raised his palms to his eyes and wiped them in an outward direction. "Lirim Jovanović is dead?" were the first words out of his expressionless mouth.

"Yes, strangled last Wednesday night," Damon replied, unsure whether the conversation was over or not.

After a pause, the sheriff pronounced, "That's fine by me." He took a small sip of coffee. "I think those rumors are true, Mr. Lassard, but I suspect there's no way to prove it now. It's something that's bothered me greatly for years."

"If you suspected it, why didn't you do anything about it?" Damon asked, then immediately regretted his candor.

But Ravi Anbani just smiled. "I wish I could have. Back then, I was still a volunteer reserve. The sheriff was Jonathan Greely. The way I remember it is that several local men came into the office over the course of about a week. And every one of them had a similar story. Lirim Jovanović had approached them about buying photos of a little girl. I mean he just flat out came up to these guys, told them he had illicit pictures and asked whether they wanted to buy any. Most of the men had children of their own, so naturally they came to us. At least some of them did. Who knows if any took Jovanović up on his offer."

"I can't believe he could be so brazen," Damon said.

"Me neither, though he didn't come out and show the men the photos. Every person who came to the office said Lirim wasn't willing to show them what he had until they gave him cash."

"Couldn't Sheriff Greely have just put someone undercover to buy a picture?"

"Mr. Lassard, I'm going to be frank with you," Anbani said. "I don't think Sheriff Greely ever did a damn thing about it. Not for real anyway." He sighed. "After the first few of these reports came in, Greely gathered the deputies and volunteers and told us that he'd be looking into the matter personally. The allegations were of grave consequence, he said, and anyone who had a complaint should be directed to him. He'd personally handle the questioning of Lirim Jovanović and all of the men who came forward. I should have known right then something was amiss. It felt wrong but I was just too green to realize why." He laid his hands on the desk. "In retrospect, I realize the tip-off should have been that Greely almost never took cases on himself. He was far too insouciant for that. I was new to the field so I try not to kick myself over it, but I do. Sometimes, in the early morning hours, I still wake up with guilt eating away at my insides."

"But shouldn't the deputies have known?" Damon asked.

"Of course they should have." Anbani banged his fist against the mahogany desktop. "Idiots. Though I don't suspect any of them did anything nefarious. They wouldn't have been smart enough to cover it up."

Damon glanced behind him toward the cracked open door. He could hear people milling about the office.

"Don't worry, they're all gone now. Either let go or finally left of their own accord when I was elected sheriff. They knew the gravy train days had come to an end. And I didn't succeed Greely directly. Sheriff in this county is an elected position, and there's a two-term limit. There were two other sheriffs between the time Greely was in office and now."

"So do you think Sheriff Greely covered for Lirim?" Damon asked focused on Anbani's masculine face.

"I do, Mr. Lassard. I can't prove it, but I do. The thing is, Greely was clever. He may have been lazy, but he knew how to get things done when they needed to be done. After he told us that he was running the investigation solo, he was out of the office for almost two weeks, interviewing witnesses and questioning Jovanović. I'm pretty sure Greely even got a search warrant for his house and the carnival trailers and other equipment that were at a nearby storage facility."

"He didn't find anything?"

"That's what he said. But just because Greely said he came up empty doesn't mean it's true."

"And no girl ever came forward," Damon said.

"I don't think so. Not even Greely would have been able to cover that up. He told the prosecutor he had nothing but unsubstantiated accounts. And from my years of experience now, I know stories that aren't backed by concrete evidence are worthless to a prosecutor. The defense counsel would just argue that a group of men had a bone to pick with the defendant and they colluded to spread a nasty rumor."

"Why would Sheriff Greely have covered for him?"

"I've asked myself that many times. The truth is I suspect he was a customer. It's possible that Jovanović had some dirt on the sheriff, or paid him off, but I think the sheriff got word that he was selling the pictures and wanted a set of his own. This all happened just before the Internet became common."

"So the deviants couldn't sit in the privacy of their basements downloading the filth," Damon said following the sheriff's line of thinking. "They had to have a physical channel of distribution."

"Exactly. And they don't sell magazines featuring pre-teens off the shelf."

"Did any of the men who reported being approached by Lirim raise a fuss after the sheriff called off the investigation?"

"I don't recall any particular protests. I suppose when the sheriff searched Jovanović's property and said he didn't find anything, the locals assumed Jovanović was just trying to get a rise out of them. Which was not Lirim's nature at all. From what I knew of the man, he rarely spoke to anyone in town. I don't think he had any friends here, even though he lived most of his life on that property in Cheat Lake. I think his parents came from Croatia or Albania when he was a boy."

Damon sipped coffee from his bright yellow mug. It was lukewarm. "Are his parents still there?"

"They both passed. Lirim had been living there with them when he married Tabitha and she moved in. The four of them lived in the house together for a few years. It's a pretty large property—about an acre and a half. But then Lirim's father died of prostate cancer and shortly after that his mother went to live in one of the assisted living facilities here in town. She died five or six years ago."

"Do you know whether Tabby knew about Sheriff Greely's investigation?" Damon asked.

"I imagine she did, though I never raised it with her or heard her speak about it with anyone—not that she was much of a talker, either."

Damon wondered whether Tabby had known. Not only of the rumors but also of the truth. And had a teenage Clara heard the rumors about her father? Or been a subject?

"And you didn't reopen the case when you became sheriff," Damon said boldly.

Anbani's face soured briefly then mellowed. "I didn't. The problem is there hasn't been a complaint in fifteen years. No judge would ever sign a search warrant."

"Too bad," Damon said, getting ready to take his leave. But then he recalled his other line of questions. "Sorry to take up so much of your time, Sheriff, but I wanted to ask you about something else, too."

The sheriff asked him to "stay put" for a minute and disappeared from the office. With the door opened wide, Damon could hear voices coming from down the hall, in the direction of the room where Ravi Anbani had retrieved their coffees a half hour earlier. Damon picked up the yellow mug from his lap. It was dripping with cold condensate. He looked down and stared in dismay at a wet spot the size of an orange near the zipper of his khaki shorts. Damon lurched for a tissue from a box on Anbani's desk. Panicked wiping made the spot double in size.

He heard Anbani's footsteps approaching the office. Damon untucked his polo shirt and quickly stretched it over his knees.

Anbani returned and sat behind his desk. He eyed Damon curiously, then noticed the yellow mug sweating on the corner of his desk.

"I wanted to ask you about Tabby's car wreck," Damon stammered.

"I can't help you much there unfortunately," the sheriff grumbled. "You'll need to speak with my deputy, Jasper Horton. I was in India when it happened. My wife's cousin was getting married and we used it as an excuse to take a three week trip to the subcontinent. It was my first real vacation since I was elected sheriff."

"Deputy Horton didn't consider it anything other than a hit-and-run?" Damon asked.

Ravi Anbani's eyes narrowed and he gave Damon a penetrating look. "Jasper didn't. And I read the reports when I returned. I didn't see anything to suggest otherwise. But reading a report is never the same as being there. Is there something you know to the contrary, Mr. Lassard?" Damon felt the other man's intensity searing across the desk and was thankful not to be a suspect on the other end of the sheriff's questioning.

"Tabby's brother Toma seemed skeptical that it was an accident. He didn't mention anything concrete to back up his belief. It may have just been a gut feeling, but it piqued my interest."

Anbani picked up a black corded telephone from his desk and punched a single digit on the system's base. The receptionist's voice came over speakerphone. "Yes Sheriff?"

"Carla, can you find the file on a Tabitha Jovanović and ask Jasper to bring it to me?" He spelled Jovanović. "But first, please bring me today's newspaper."

The receptionist entered and handed Anbani a thick *Dominion Post*. The sheriff pulled off the top two sections and handed them to Damon. "I thought you might want to know what kind of spills we get to clean up around here," Anbani said with a wink as an embarrassed but grateful Damon placed the paper on his lap and unwound his shirt from his knees.

The sheriff shifted gears. "How much about Lirim's past do the Arlington police know?"

Damon admitted that he hadn't yet told them about the child pornography rumors he heard the previous evening. "I wanted to speak with you first to verify the veracity of the rumors before sending the detectives down a wrong path."

The sheriff didn't opine on the wisdom of that decision but rather requested the names and phone numbers of the detectives on the case, which Damon provided.

A moment later, a young man close in age to Damon knocked at Anbani's open door. Jasper Horton was tall and thin with a shock of wavy blond hair. He handed the sheriff a thin folder.

"Jasper, Mr. Lassard and I want to walk through this car accident," the sheriff said holding up the file folder.

Jasper Horton didn't question Damon's interest in the matter. He scratched the underside of his chin, which was dotted with stubble. "That was almost a year and a half ago. In December, I believe. Woman in her mid- to late-fifties. Dark green car, though I can't remember the make offhand. It should be in the file."

"Forest green Cavalier," Anbani said peering down at the open file folder.

"That's right," replied Horton. "An older model. The woman hadn't been wearing her seat belt so even though the airbag deployed, it wasn't much help. In fact, the airbag probably killed her."

Damon gave the deputy an inquisitive look.

"You don't want to hit an airbag while it's still inflating," Horton said. "You want the bag to be in the deflation stage, through the airbag's vents, by the time the driver makes impact. A deflating bag will cushion the head and neck. If it's still inflating on impact, it's like hitting your head against a brick wall." The deputy straightened his posture. "It can crush your spine right along the back of your neck. That's why a seat belt is so important. Without one, your head is much more likely to smash up against the airbag while it's inflating rather than deflating. And that woman Tabitha's spine looked like a row of knocked over dominoes under her skin."

Sheriff Anbani looked up from the file folder. "Enough physics lessons, Horton. Impressive, though."

The deputy tried to suppress a smile. The young man clearly had aspirations.

The sheriff asked, "Do you know whether Tabby Jovanović usually wore her seat belt?"

Horton was caught off guard and looked at the floor. "I don't," he mumbled. "I didn't think to ask about that."

Anbani didn't chastise the young deputy. Why would Horton have questioned it if the incident looked like a clear cut hit-and-run? Rather, Anbani asked, "Any idea of what a fifty-something-year-old woman was doing on the road in the middle of the night?"

"I don't," Horton answered. "Neither did the husband. He said they had gone to bed together that night, so who knows. Maybe she couldn't fall asleep and wanted to take a drive. Or maybe she was sneaking out behind her husband's back."

Damon considered the latter explanation. Lirim was on the road a majority of the year, so it would have been very easy for Tabby to have an affair. But the accident was in December while Lirim was staying in Morgantown. Maybe she couldn't hold off until spring and had gone to meet a paramour under the cover of night. It was exactly what her daughter had done.

Damon directed his attention to Jasper Horton. "I read in the newspaper that the car had the majority of its damage on the front driver's corner, as if it was in a head-on collision."

"That's right," Jasper said. "There were black paint marks at the impact location, and the vehicle that hit the Cavalier must have been much larger and going fast because it pushed the Cavalier into the ditch."

"Any footprints?" asked the sheriff.

"None that we saw," Jasper said defensively. "But I'm fairly certain we'd been going through a dry spell, so even if the other driver had gotten out of his vehicle, footprints wouldn't have shown up too well on the gravel. And you know how those roads are, Sheriff. There are tire tracks everywhere and you can't tell which ones are the freshest if there's no moisture on the ground."

"That's a pity," the sheriff said.

Jasper turned in his chair to face Damon. "So do you think this was something other than a hit-and-run? Like someone ran her down on purpose?"

"I really don't know, but that's exactly what I was wondering. Tabby left a decent-sized estate. The principal was untouchable while she was alive. Her husband, brother and daughter each claimed a share after she died."

"I questioned the husband," Jasper said. "He seemed pretty shaken up."

Damon couldn't think of any further questions. He rose and shook hands with each of the officers.

"I appreciate you coming by, Mr. Lassard," Sheriff Anbani said. "I'll give the Arlington detectives a call and fill them in." He glanced down at the *Post* Damon held shielding his shorts. "Feel free to keep the paper."

Chapter 13

After changing at the hotel, Damon picked up nourishment from a local bagel shop.

He left Gerry a message, first apologizing for making the trip to Pennsylvania and West Virginia without telling him, and then filling him in on the events of his morning and previous evening. Finally, he relayed that Sheriff Anbani from Monongalia County, West Virginia, would be calling either him or Lieutenant Hobbes.

Damon considered Lirim's photographs. Digital cameras that could be connected to a printer hadn't been commonplace at the time, so either Lirim knew how to develop pictures or was working with someone who did. Damon longed to search Lirim's property—there could be a darkroom on site right now if he continued to sell photos on the road after he ceased harassing the locals. He conjured the image of a disused carnival trailer sitting at the rear of the property that doubled as a photography studio and darkroom.

Damon decided against nosing around within the bounds of Lirim's property. He might unknowingly alter critical evidence. But that didn't stop him from taking a peek from the road.

Damon drove outside the city limits. Paved streets turned to gravel. Damon was no stranger to this type of road—rural Michigan was littered with them. Gravel roads had been a favorite topic of conversation with his maternal grandfather who had lived fifty miles north of Detroit.

The gravel roads near Morgantown were recently graded and smooth. But as soon as Damon turned left onto Railback Road, where the Jovanović family had resided for decades, he hit a rutted "washboard" surface. He hadn't thought to ask Jasper Horton about the condition of the road surface where Tabby was killed. An unlit road as corrugated as Railback was this afternoon could easily throw a driver off course if he or she was drunk or just not paying attention.

Damon found Lirim's property without difficulty. A mailbox fashioned in the style of a boxy brown birdhouse at the end of a twenty-yard curving driveway revealed the address in white block characters. He parked his Saab alongside a deep roadside ditch across from the Jovanović family home.

Damon stared at the derelict house. It was a single-story clapboard-sided structure that would have been described as Cape Cod style in Arlington's upscale real estate guides. But here in the rural outskirts of a mid-sized West Virginia town, the home was a flat-fronted domicile devoid of external care or visible foliage. Damon recalled Jim Riley telling him that Tabby cleaned Lirim's fairground trailer every summer and wondered how much decay had set into the Cheat Lake home during the eighteen months since her death. The large grass front yard, yellow from the summer's heat, contrasted with an unattractive stain on the house's weather-worn siding comparable in color to the shade of the pea green sofa in Lirim's trailer.

Where had the interest from Tabitha's trust been spent? Certainly not on her home's exterior. Damon did some mental calculations. Clara said a one-third share of Tabby's estate was one hundred and fifty thousand dollars. Interest payments at six percent on four hundred and fifty thousand dollars would have given Tabby an annual pre-tax income of twenty seven thousand. It was enough to live on, but that was about all.

He had assumed that Lirim and Tabby shared their earnings, but maybe that wasn't the case. Clara's grandfather probably made a wise decision to disallow the trust's principal to be touched during Tabby's lifetime out of fear that Lirim would have found a way to get his hands on it. On the other hand, it created a motive for three people to cut her days short. One hundred and fifty thousand dollars wasn't a Powerball win, but it was more than enough money to solve a lot of problems.

The driveway split at the end of the curve, with the right tine of the two-pronged fork abruptly dead-ending at a doorless side of the house. The left tine, spotted with dense thatches of weeds, led to a large free-standing building with a two-car garage door at its front—the "shed" Lirim referred to in his opinion letter. From his perspective twenty yards away, Damon thought it looked self-constructed. Between the house and garage, a large open space continued for some distance before backing into woodlands. A handful of cast-off carnival structures were barely visible in varying degrees of intactness.

On the far side of the road from the house, deciduous trees edged right up to the ditch. Fifty feet further down, he could make out the opening of a driveway cutting into the woods. And in the several hundred yards he had driven on Railback Road, Damon had only passed a single other home.

Damon walked in the direction of the opening into the woods. He reasoned that talking to a neighbor would be less intrusive than speaking to the sheriff, which he had already done. The driveway that appeared was long and narrow, flanked on either side by towering hardwoods. From the end, Damon couldn't see a house—the drive veered uphill to the right and disappeared. He trudged up the steep gradient. His calves voiced their disagreement. Gravel turned to asphalt when Damon rounded the curve and saw a classic Tudor house significantly larger and in better condition than the Jovanović residence.

Set back in the woods, it had a small front yard that was neatly landscaped, presumably by the man on his knees with his backside raised in the air and stabbing at the ground with a gardening implement. An eager male voice emanated from a decades-old boom box, loudly criticizing the Pittsburgh Pirates' relief pitching. As soon as Damon turned from the driveway onto a walkway, the man wheeled around on his knees and raised the handheld tool. It featured a straight sharp blade for excavating roots. Damon stepped back and held up both hands. The man took in Damon's neatly groomed features and collared shirt. He relaxed his grip on the tool, but didn't set it down.

"Is there something I can do for you, son?" he asked in a manner that was neither threatening nor welcoming. Damon judged him to be in his early seventies with a shrewd face and a light complexion reddened by the sun.

Damon introduced himself. "I'm trying to find out more about your neighbor across the road," Damon said. "Lirim Jovanović."

"What about him?" the man responded with caution.

"He was murdered in Virginia a few days ago."

"Murdered," he repeated. "That doesn't sound pleasant. Are you with police?"

"I'm not," Damon admitted. "A friend of mine is a detective there handling the case and I've just come from speaking with Sheriff Anbani."

His face softened at the mention of the sheriff's name. "Anbani's a good man. Hard worker, upstanding guy. Did he ask you to come out here?"

"No," Damon confessed. "I'm the president of a citizens association out east and he was killed at my fairgrounds. I'm just trying to get some peace."

The man weighed the pros and cons of divulging his thoughts about Lirim, then opted to keep his mouth closed. "Sorry, son. You seem nice enough, but I just don't know you. Not too many people come up my driveway, even fewer on foot. And no good has ever come of anyone who did. But if you come back with the sheriff, I won't shut the door on you."

Damon thanked him, retreated down the driveway and drove the Saab to the first home he had passed on the Jovanović side of Railback Road. He parked in front of a white picket fence that hadn't seen a coat of paint in decades. The house was a dusty, two-story, unadorned wooden structure that a single cigarette butt could burn to the ground in minutes.

If he was unsuccessful at this home, Damon would tuck his tail between his legs and return to Hollydale. He rapped at the front door and waited for thirty seconds. He was about to turn away when he heard light shuffling sounds from inside. After another twenty seconds of patient waiting, a timid female voice shrilled, "Who's there?"

Rather than commence a one-sided dialogue about murder through a solid oak door, Damon said he was a friend of Clara Jovanović's and he had some information about her family to pass along. At the mention of Clara's name, a bolt turned and the door opened slowly. Facing him was a woman about his mother's age, but that's where the similarity ended. The large-boned woman standing in a bleak alcove had a hunched posture and downcast eyes.

Without speaking, she gestured Damon inside and led him through a dark hallway to a modest sitting room. Heavy curtains were drawn tightly and the space was dimly lit by low-wattage lamps. A fish tank caked with algae dominated one wall. The woman quietly introduced herself as Johnnetta Frank and offered Damon hot tea. He politely declined and waited until she had seated herself in a white wicker rocker before choosing a faded black chair bearing the logo of Duquesne University.

"My husband loved that chair," she said. "He attended university there and talked about it until the day he died."

"I'm very sorry to hear that he's passed on," Damon replied. He felt like he was at a wake at that very moment. "Mrs. Frank. I have some news about your neighbor and also wanted to ask you a few questions, if you don't mind," Damon said.

"Depends on the questions, I suppose," she responded, folding her hands in her lap. "But go ahead."

"I'm not quite sure how to say this, except to come right out with it. Your neighbor Lirim Jovanović died earlier in the week. He was murdered."

Johnnetta Frank's expression was one of relief mixed with fear. "Thank the Lord," she finally said, casting her eyes to the ceiling.

Damon reflected on how uniformly those who knew Lirim appeared to relish his death. Johnnetta's reaction bolstered his confidence and he asked for her thoughts on the man.

"Rotten right to the core, he was. I don't know how Tabby put up with him, much less stayed with him. He didn't give her a red cent. If she hadn't had a bit of money of her own, she would have starved to death."

"So you and Mrs. Jovanović were close, I gather," Damon said.

"Close as sisters," she replied, her voice gaining strength. "My husband died eight years ago and Lirim was on the road half of the time, so we kept each other company."

"It must be tough now," Damon said neutrally, trying to find an opening into her thoughts on Tabby's accident.

"The days do go by more slowly now that Tabby's not around."

"Maybe Clara will sell the home now and the new neighbors will be friendly," Damon said with genuine optimism in his voice.

"Anything would be an improvement over that louse Lirim," she replied, inching her face forward toward Damon.

Damon took advantage of the intimacy, leaned in himself, and asked conspiratorially, "Have you heard anything about Lirim taking pictures of young girls?"

Johnnetta hesitated, unsure of whether to confide in him. She started to cross her legs, but thought better of it in the company of a man whom she had just met, even though her skirt swept below her ankles. "Of course I heard," she said timidly. "Everyone heard about it, including Tabby. She was mortified."

"Did Clara know, too?"

"I certainly hope not. My husband and I certainly never mentioned the subject in her presence."

"Did Tabby confront Lirim about the pictures?" Damon pressed.

She paused again then went to the nearby kitchen and returned with a glass tumbler filled with a yellowish-brown liquid that smelled of lemon tea with honey. She sat back down, carefully balancing the glass with both hands in her lap. Finally, she spoke. "I don't know whether Tabby confronted Lirim fifteen years ago when the rumors were going around and Sheriff Greely came to their house. But I think she did a year and a half ago."

Damon leaned in again. "Was he still taking photos?"

"No, no. I think he stopped almost as soon as he started. There was only ever one girl and one photo session. At least that's what Tabby told me." Damon felt the hairs on the back of his neck begin to itch. He didn't interrupt.

"She found a stash of pictures. Less than two weeks before her accident. Lirim had gone on a weekend fishing trip and Tabby decided to give the garage a thorough scrubbing. She rarely went into the garage because they didn't keep cars in there. It was strictly used for Lirim's equipment."

Johnnetta winced. "About four hours into cleaning, she was pulling things down from a set of shelves to dust underneath. From the top shelf she removed a flat metal box, like one that would hold a ratchet set. When she was climbing down the stepladder she noticed how light it was. Tabby said it just struck her as feeling strange—a box for tools should have been heavy. So she snapped the container open."

Johnnetta's hands trembled and she tipped her tumbler of tea. Warm liquid splashed onto her floor length cotton skirt. Damon strode quickly into the narrow galley kitchen and found a roll of paper towels. He handed them to Johnnetta and she adroitly dabbed at her lap.

"Sorry about that," she stammered nervously.

"It's quite all right, Mrs. Frank. Can I get you a fresh glass of tea?"

"No, no. I'm all right." She set the stemless glass on the coffee table between a faded wedding album and an empty tissue box. "I can go on. It's high time I talked to someone about this. I only wish my Frederick had still been alive when Tabby told me. He would have known what to do."

She continued. "As you can guess, the metal box contained pictures of a little girl without clothing. Originals and copies. I never saw them but Tabby said the girl couldn't have been more than ten or eleven years old. She said there was nothing seductive about them. It was just a white-skinned bare child standing up straight, sitting cross-legged and lying down, but not sexually positioned."

"Did Tabby know who the girl was?"

"She said she didn't. It wasn't Clara, if that's what you're thinking. I know because I asked Tabby point blank and she said no." Johnnetta Frank crossed herself. "And these weren't professional photographs, either. They were instant shots from a Polaroid. In color, but crude. I think Lirim had about twenty pictures and made copies of them. Those must have been what he was selling."

"Copies of an instant photo?" Damon asked.

"Tabby said it looked like the Polaroids were laid down on the face of a copy machine and just copied onto plain paper."

"You said Tabby confronted Lirim. Was that right after she found the photos?"

"It was. Lirim was on his trip until the following day and Tabby didn't want to discuss the matter over the telephone. So she came to see me and told me what she found. She said she had believed her husband all of those years ago. At the time, he said a group of men made up a story because he had beaten them out of some money at a poker game. And after Sheriff Greely came to speak with Lirim and looked around the house, the sheriff's office dropped the inquiry. So she thought she had done right by him to believe in him."

Johnnetta started to reach for her tea, then realized the tumbler was empty. "I remember the day she told me like it was yesterday. We sat right here, and she cried and cried. It didn't surprise me that she found those pictures. My Frederick never liked Lirim Jovanović. Said he was a bad seed. After she stopped crying, she told me she was going to confront him and wave the pictures in his face. 'And then what?' I asked. She didn't want to tell the sheriff if she was convinced it was an isolated incident because it would have been too shameful to have the police and television reporters all over her house. Instead, she said she would play her trump card and tell the heathen she was cutting him out of her will."

Damon nodded and urged her to continue. He still didn't know how the pieces fit together, but they were starting to stack up.

"Tabby and Lirim were about the same age but smoking had blackened her lungs. Lirim figured he would outlive her by a good many years, so removing him from her will would have come as a blow. Do you know about Tabby's trust?"

Damon said that he did and that Tabby Jovanović must not have changed the terms of her will in time because Lirim received his share from the liquidated trust.

"What a shame that car accident was," Johnnetta said with sympathy. "For as long as I live, I'll never understand what she was doing on the road in the middle of the night."

"And you didn't hear her car leave," Damon posited.

"No. I'm a sound sleeper and the woods between our houses deadens all of the sound."

Damon remembered the question that Sheriff Anbani had asked of Jasper Horton. "Mrs. Frank, did Tabby typically wear her seat belt?"

She responded in a patronizing voice one might reserve for a child. "Yes, she always did."

Damon changed course. "Did you ever tell anyone what Tabby told you about the pictures?" he asked gently.

Johnnetta cast her eyes down to the floor to avert his gaze. "No," she said in a mild tone. "I haven't told anyone until now."

Damon felt as if the middle-aged woman wasn't being completely truthful with him. He didn't want to push her but felt compelled to ask why she hadn't told the sheriff about Tabby's discovery after the car accident.

"I don't know," she responded. "It's not in my nature to interfere, and I guess I thought it didn't matter anymore. Maybe they could have found that little girl. She'd be all grown up now. But why would a young woman in the prime of her life want to dredge up such ugly memories?"

To put the pervert who photographed her, sold naked pictures of her and did God knows what else to her behind bars, Damon thought. But instead of expressing that notion, he rose from his chair and thanked Johnnetta Frank for her time.

As she walked with him to the front door she asked, "Will the sheriff come to talk with me?"

"I expect he will." Damon stepped onto the walkway in front of the house. "But now that Lirim's dead, I can't imagine he'll have too many questions."

Chapter 14

Damon had confirmed that Lirim Jovanović exploited a young girl. He didn't know how it tied to Lirim's death, but it was a significant advancement. He needed to call Gerry and Sheriff Anbani to alert them of his discovery. Back at the Hampton Inn, he turned on his phone and retrieved a message from Gerry. He had spoken with Sheriff Anbani about the rumors of Lirim's child pornography distribution endeavor. Clara, now the rightful owner of the Jovanović home on Railback Road, had consented to a search of the premises. Gerry was on the road and meeting Anbani in front of the house at three thirty that afternoon.

Damon looked down at his watch. It was just past one. He booked in for a second night and then called Ravi Anbani and relayed the information passed to him by Johnnetta Frank. Damon could sense the sheriff's excitement over the telephone. Anbani would speak with Johnnetta Frank before meeting Gerry Sloman that afternoon.

Damon hesitated before calling Gerry. He felt guilty for pursuing inquiries on his own. He wasn't qualified to conduct an investigation. But he was achieving results and that felt good. Damon was also concerned about Margaret Hobbes' reaction to the news of Damon making his own inquiries. He didn't want Gerry's superior officer to blame the detective just because the two men were friends.

Damon was able to reach Gerry on his mobile and passed the latest information along to him. He couldn't tell whether Gerry was pleased with his detecting or annoyed by the interference. For all Damon knew, photographing the girl was a one-time incident more than a decade old and Damon's discovery was taking Gerry away from finding Lirim's real murderer. But still, he had found something tangible for the police to sink their teeth into and it made him feel proud.

Damon took a mid-afternoon nap and was back on Railback Road at three-thirty. He pulled in behind Sheriff Anbani, who was stepping out of his vehicle. Gerry Sloman was already there, leaning against a broad-leafed oak tree on the other side of the ditch, peering at a handheld device. Damon introduced the men, who shook hands.

"You made good time," Damon said to Gerry.

Gerry responded genially but then turned his attention to the sheriff from West Virginia. "I have permission from Lirim's daughter to go onto the premises and into all of the structures. No restrictions."

"Good," Anbani said. He spoke just as formally as Gerry. "I just came from the neighbor's house. Johnnetta Frank confirmed the story she told Damon this morning." He consulted his wristwatch. "We have about five hours of light left. The house isn't very big, but there's the garage and a decent amount of land. Do you want me to call in a deputy or two?"

Damon looked at the men standing before him. Neither was willing to meet his gaze. It was clear that Damon wasn't going to be invited to participate in the search. He was disappointed—neither man would have been there if not for his intuition. But he assumed there could be evidentiary problems if he found something useful.

"Let's start and make a decision in an hour on whether we need more bodies," Gerry said to Anbani.

Gerry turned to face Damon. "Sorry Damon, we can't let you come in with us," he said. "I'm appreciative of the information you've uncovered. But you're not an officer of the law." Gerry turned away with an apologetic look—he knew Damon had been trying to help and succeeding.

Damon drove to a restaurant called "Bobby's Burgers" at the end of a strip mall near his hotel and ventured inside. The place was deserted save for two attractive women eating salads and drinking from matching cans of Fanta Zero. He ordered a regular Fanta along with a half-pound cheeseburger and a basket of fries.

He selected a booth that had a discarded newspaper in it and decided to wait out Gerry and Ravi Anbani.

Two hours and three sodas later, a call came in from Gerry.

"Jackpot!" he exclaimed.

"You found the pictures?" Damon asked with energy.

"Photocopies. And here's the best part—Anbani says he knows who the girl is. We're heading back to the sheriff's office. Meet us there in fifteen minutes. Anbani's sending in his deputies to finish the search."

The gatekeeper Carla had been replaced behind the sheriff's office front desk by a pencil thin man. He led Damon to Sheriff Anbani's office.

Anbani pointed Damon to the same chair he had been seated in hours earlier. Gerry Sloman occupied the seat that had been occupied by Deputy Horton. Gerry's eyes were brimming with enthusiasm despite the weary slouch of his body.

"I can't believe the old bugger still had them," Gerry said. "After all of this time and after his wife caught him red-handed."

"Did you find the originals?" Damon asked.

Anbani responded. "No, they're a set of paper photocopies. My deputies are tearing the place apart looking for the originals, tough Tabitha probably destroyed those after she found them."

"Mrs. Frank suggested that there were about twenty different photographs," Gerry said. "We only found photocopies of six. All of the same girl and very poor quality."

"We'll need to contact some of the carnival folks to see if Lirim was still in the sales business," Anbani said. "But we doubt it after all of this time and with such old pictures."

"Where did you find them?" Damon asked Gerry.

"In his bedroom. Hardly hidden at all." Gerry smiled. "We started with the garage because that was where Tabby found Lirim's main stash. We found a switchblade and a pretty severe looking hunting knife in the bottom of a wastepaper basket full of rags, but no pictures."

Ravi Anbani took up the discourse. "Then we searched the house. That place is disgusting inside. It probably hasn't been cleaned since Tabitha died. There are ants parading all over the dining room floor and the whole kitchen stinks of decayed chicken. We left those areas to the deputies." He grinned widely and Damon pictured Jasper Horton donning a disposable face mask as he pawed through rotten hulks of unidentifiable food.

"But the pictures were in the bedroom," Anbani continued. "He had a brown leather briefcase with real brass rivets. Inside was a tattered manila envelope with the photocopies." The sheriff picked up an envelope matching the description from his desk and waved it triumphantly. "I knew that son of a bitch was guilty. I only wish I could have done something about it when he was alive. You sure you want to find his killer, Detective?" The older lawman gave Gerry a wink.

"I'm sure," Gerry said. "Jovanović doesn't have an exclusive license on being an asshole."

Ravi Anbani left the office and came back with three bottles of water. Taking one from his rough skinned hand, Damon asked, "So you think you know who the girl is?"

"I do," Anbani said, standing in the narrow gap between the wall behind his desk and his black mesh swivel chair. "I have a daughter. She's in college now, but about ten years ago, she spent two weeks at an all-day summer art camp down I-79 in Fairmont. That's about twenty miles southwest of here. My wife was still working then so we had to find somewhere for Hayden to spend the daytime hours." He looked down at the framed picture of his family on the front of his desk. "I happened to be spending most of my summer down in Fairmont. The Marion County sheriff who is based down there had taken ill and they didn't have an experienced deputy to step into the role. So I volunteered and spent two months testing my chops at the top position."

He took a lengthy drink from his water bottle and sat down in his desk chair. "Hayden's instructor was a woman in her thirties. A single mother who taught courses through the Fairmont Parks and Recreation department. She brought her teenage daughter to class with her every day to serve as her assistant. I remember Hayden really liked the girl—she wore fashionable jeans. I saw the teacher and her daughter every day for two weeks and I am positive the daughter is the girl in Jovanović's photos."

"That would have been about five years after the pictures were taken," Damon said.

"That's right," Anbani said. "And even though I haven't thought about that girl in the ten years since the end of Hayden's art camp, I definitely recognize her."

"So now what?" asked Damon. "Do you remember her name or her mother's name?"

"No, but I might be able to find out," Anbani said to Damon while winking at Gerry. That was the second wink of the meeting. Damon had the impression the two of them had agreed to allow Damon to participate as a way of repaying him for finding out about Lirim's sordid past.

Anbani picked up the landline receiver from the telephone base on his neatly kept desk.

"Are you calling your daughter?" Damon asked.

"Better. The sheriff down in Marion County." The ringing from the other end of the line was audible. No one answered and Ravi Anbani touched the dial tone button and punched in another number. This time it connected and after thirty seconds of conversation he hung up. "I caught the sheriff on his home phone. He's finding the number for the director of the Fairmont Parks and Recreation Department."

The telephone rang a minute later and the sheriff scrawled a number on a clean sheet of white paper attached to a clipboard. He dialed again, this time using the speaker function.

A woman picked up and, after Anbani stressed the urgency of the call, went to interrupt her husband's shower.

Silence filled the air, save for a faint noise over the phone that sounded like a cat scratching at a post.

"Do you have any pets, Sheriff?" Damon asked, breaking the quiet.

"My wife has a cat," he said. "She sleeps on a pillow right between us on the bed." Anbani paused, then said with a coarse smile. "My wife has always had a soft spot for the cat."

A hoarse male voice came on the line.

"Lester Jackson here."

"Hi, Lester. This is Ravi Anbani, the sheriff up in Monongalia County. Sheriff Craig gave me your name and number. Sorry to interrupt you."

"No problem, Sheriff. What do you need?"

"I'm looking for a woman who taught art classes at the Fairmont Parks and Recreation Department about ten years ago."

"Not too many people stay that long, but a few do. I have an address list if you have her name."

"Unfortunately, I don't. It's actually the daughter I'm interested in, but I think finding the mother might be easier. The woman was single at the time and would probably be in her forties by now. She was of medium height, and when I saw her ten years ago, thin as a rail with long brown hair that she always wore in a ponytail. And she had a speech impediment."

Lester Jackson cut in. "Vicky Roscoph." He spelled it out. "And her daughter's name is Hannah."

Damon and Gerry looked at each other. They had a name to go with the photographs.

"Is Vicky still teaching classes down there?" Anbani asked.

"No. I'm pretty sure she and her daughter are both in Oakland, California. Hannah left Fairmont about two years after high school. Vicky went on for months about how she was all alone because her only child had moved across the country. Then, about a year ago, Vicky told me not to sign her up to teach any more classes because she was moving to live with Hannah in Oakland."

"This is absolute gold for me," Anbani said. "You wouldn't happen to have a forwarding address or telephone number would you?"

"Give me a minute. I have my work computer at home. I'll check the list." In less than two minutes Lester Jackson came back on the line. "Sorry, Sheriff, I don't have it."

"That's all right. This is still phenomenal information. If you ever need anything up here in Monongalia County, don't hesitate to call on me. And sorry about getting you out of the shower."

Chapter 15

Ravi Anbani smiled broadly at the two men from Arlington. Damon noticed for the first time how white the sheriff's teeth were.

"With an unusual name like Roscoph, she shouldn't be hard to track down if the number's listed," Gerry said.

"I'm looking it up as we speak," Anbani replied, pecking at his desktop computer. "H. Roscoph on 84th Avenue. That's the only listing."

Anbani's finger hovered above the telephone console. "Damon, if I hadn't been looking to bust Lirim Jovanović since the day I first heard about him peddling pictures, I'd never let you stay. But I am grateful to you for finding a route to the truth. Just keep quiet. Actually, why don't you both stay silent while I talk? I don't want to scare her off. Then, Gerry, if you need to follow up with her, you can make a separate call."

Damon and Gerry nodded their heads in agreement and Anbani called using the speakerphone function.

A female voice answered on the third ring. "Hello?"

"Good evening ma'am, I'm looking for Ms. Hannah Roscoph," Anbani said formally.

"This is Hannah, who's calling?" Her voice sounded wary of the sheriff's stiff tone.

"This is Sheriff Ravi Anbani from Monongalia County, West Virginia. You used to live in Fairmont, correct?"

The line went silent. Damon thought this was the moment of truth. Would she bear her soul to a sheriff on the other side of the country?

Finally, she broke the quiet. "What do you want from me?"

"To give you some information and ask you some questions. First, the information." The sheriff didn't wait for affirmation and just ripped off the bandage. "Lirim Jovanović is dead. He was strangled to death last week."

Silence again. Then a sharp intake of breath.

Anbani continued. "You and I met ten years ago, Hannah. You were assisting your mother at a summer art class in one of the Fairmont community centers. My daughter Hayden was a student in your class. She was ten. An Indian girl."

"I don't remember," she retorted.

"It doesn't matter. It was only a two-week class and that must feel like ages ago to you. But you do know who Lirim Jovanović is, don't you?"

"Yes," she said, her courage mounting. "But don't you want to talk to my mother? She's the one who dated him."

Damon shifted uncomfortably in his seat. Anbani's telephone demeanor waivered. "Your mother dated Lirim Jovanović," he repeated. "When was that?"

Hannah picked up on the modest change in intonation. "You didn't know," she said nervously, now certain why the sheriff had called.

"I didn't. But I still want to speak with you."

"Hold on, let me shut the door." The men could hear the sound of weight shifting off of a creaking bed and padded feet crossing a wooden floor.

Ten seconds later she came back on the line and spoke softly but with anger. "Lirim dated my mother for six months before she found out he was married. It must have been close to fifteen years ago."

"He pretended he wasn't married?" the sheriff asked. Damon admired his skill. The structure of the sheriff's statement squarely aligned his sentiment with Hannah Roscoph's.

"He never wore a wedding band and he was over our house in Fairmont all of the time," she said. "He made excuses about how shabby his place was and said that our house was much nicer. But eventually my mother got suspicious and followed him home."

"Did she confront him?"

"No. She found out where he lived and went back a couple of days later when she knew Lirim wouldn't be there. A woman came out of the house, and my mother followed her to a shoe store in Morgantown. The clerk appeared to know the woman, so after she left the store, my mother spoke to the salesperson and found out she was married to Lirim."

Anbani rose, walked behind his seat and gripped the chair's back. He leaned into it to stretch his lower back. "She told you all of this when you were still a child?"

"No," Hannah said. "I asked her about him just before I left Fairmont."

Anbani cracked his knuckles and took his best shot. "Hannah, I have to ask you something personal. Something uncomfortable." He paused. "Did Lirim Jovanović ever do anything inappropriate with you?"

She was anticipating the question and answered with false bravado. "He never raped me or molested me," she said.

Damon felt relief, even if it didn't lessen the impact of the violation Hannah incurred.

The sheriff retained his calm bearing. "Molestation isn't limited to physical contact, Hannah," he said delicately.

Damon could sense an emotional deflation on the other end of the line. He felt terrible for Hannah Roscoph. This woman didn't want to relive the horrendous childhood experience foisted on her by Lirim Jovanović, and now here they were, pushing her to do just that.

She gave in. "You know about the pictures." It was stated as a fact.

"Yes," Anbani said. "I know about them, and a detective and I found a set of photocopies that was still in his house."

She pretended to laugh, but it came out as more of a whimper.

"Can you tell us exactly what happened, Hannah?" Anbani asked.

"That depends," she said. "Can you protect me and my mother from the other guy?"

The three men looked at each other with anticipation.

"We can protect you if you tell us who he is." The sheriff asked and picked up a ballpoint pen to take notes.

"Victor somebody," she said without hesitation. "It was fifteen years ago, but I can still picture him. Ugly man, with beefy shoulders and fingernails chewed to the nubs."

Damon and Gerry silently sprang from their chairs in unison. Gerry grabbed a pen from his shirt pocket and scribbled furiously on Anbani's pad. "Victor McElroy. Lirim's accountant. We can get him."

The sheriff read the upside down note and spoke into the air above the speakerphone. "Is that a Victor McElroy?" he asked.

"I don't remember his last name," Hannah said. "I'm not sure I ever knew it. But I'm sure I could recognize him if you scanned me his picture."

Anbani took down her e-mail address and promised to send a photo as soon as he had one.

"And you'll protect me and my mother from him?" she asked.

"He'll be behind bars tonight, and we'll coordinate with the Oakland police to make sure you both stay safe from him," the sheriff said. He explained that most child abuse offenses in West Virginia didn't have statutes of limitations. Meanwhile, Gerry jerked a phone from his jacket pocket and left the room.

At Ravi Anbani's insistence, Hannah agreed to allow him to turn on a recording device to get the details on tape. By the time Anbani had spoken the necessary background information into the recorder for evidentiary support, Gerry returned and slid a note onto the desk—he put in a request for the police in Victor's hometown of Front Royal to arrest and hold him.

Hannah began her repulsive narrative. "I was in fifth grade when Lirim started seeing my mother. She met him in Fairmont. My mother is a free spirit and had a pretty voracious appetite for sex. I remember when I was in second grade, all of my friends were jealous because I had a television set in my room. Whenever my mother had company, she let me watch a movie with the lights off and the volume turned way up, like I was in a theater. Of course, years later I realized why, but at the time I just enjoyed it. Don't get me wrong, she wasn't selling her body, she just enjoyed the company of men." Hannah coughed.

"Lirim always came to our house, but he was never interested in me. I was usually doing homework or playing video games in my room. The three of us ate dinner together once in a while, but he didn't say more than a few words to me. After my mother found out he was married and broke it off with him, I didn't see him for another six months."

She paused and the sheriff said, "This is great, Hannah. Thank you. Please take all of the time you need."

Encouraged, she continued. "By the time I saw Lirim again I had just turned eleven and was in sixth grade. My mother was teaching classes at the rec center in the late afternoons, so I was home alone for about three hours after school every day. It never crossed my mind to lock the front door. That day, I was in my bedroom with the radio on and I never even heard him enter."

Hannah sniffed. Damon pictured a courageous young woman on her bed in a small apartment struggling to choke back tears. Tears of his own had started to well in his eyes.

"He didn't hit me or tie me up or anything. But he told me that I had to come with him and showed me a knife. It looked like a hunting knife. He said I would be back in less than two hours, before my mother came home. He didn't blindfold me or shove me into a trunk or anything like that. I sat beside him in an old junky car, and he drove about fifteen minutes outside of town. I remember thinking he was going to rape me. Even at eleven years old I knew what rape was." She had been trying to restrain her tears but now she let them out freely, but quietly. Damon assumed she had never told Vicky Roscoph and didn't want her mother to find out.

"I was crying so hard that I never thought to jump out of the car at a stoplight or to open the window and scream. Of course, we lived pretty close to the edge of town and you know how rural it is, Sheriff. After a couple of minutes, we didn't pass many other cars. He took me to a mobile home in the parking lot of an abandoned airfield."

She stopped to blow her nose and Anbani encouraged her to take her time.

Damon heard a distant voice over the other end of the speakerphone. Hannah stopped. "Hold on, Sheriff. I have to get my mother something."

Anbani pressed the pause button on the recorder and muted the telephone.

"So you know the accomplice?" the sheriff asked Gerry.

"Yes, he's been working for Lirim's carnival company. But Lirim's partner, Jim Riley, fired him a few days ago. Lirim and Victor had been skimming money from the proceeds."

"Why didn't Mr. Riley go to the police?" the sheriff asked.

"We're still not sure," Gerry admitted. "There's something Jim isn't telling us."

"Interesting. But you can find Victor McElroy?"

"Yes," Gerry confirmed. "As long as he didn't run." He paused in contemplation. "He gave us a home address. So we think we know where he lives."

"I hope so," interjected Damon, feeling left out of the conversation. "If not, Jim Riley might have the right address. I'm sure the traveling carnival keeps meticulous records." All three men broke the tension with nervous laughter, in spite of the terrible joke.

A moment later they heard the bedroom door shut over the speakerphone. After Ravi Anbani restarted the recorder, Hannah resumed her account.

"Victor was waiting for us in the mobile home. He didn't say much, but Lirim told me his name. I suppose he was trying to make me feel more comfortable. Lirim held out the knife and told me to take off my clothes. Neither he nor Victor ever actually touched me. Thank God for small miracles."

Hannah began to cry even more liberally. Damon could hear her pulling tissues out of a box and wiping them against her face.

"Lirim said that some of the men he knew on the carnival circuit would pay him for pictures of a naked girl. Not like the ones in *Playboy* or *Penthouse*. Those are women, he said. Even the barely legal magazines at the newsstands were mostly girls in their late teens. He had a couple of customers lined up for pictures of a ten- or eleven-year-old girl. And since he knew my schedule and my mother's schedule, I must have been the perfect candidate. They didn't make me touch myself or do anything obscene. I don't think Lirim or Victor had any interest in an eleven-year-old girl sexually. They acted very businesslike—they saw an opportunity to make money and were taking it. I was scared, so I did what they asked. I took off my clothes and laid on a bed and stood and sat in four or five different poses and that was it. Victor took pictures with an instant camera while Lirim read a newspaper."

"Afterwards, Lirim gave me a can of Coca Cola and drove me home. We didn't speak during the car ride, but when he dropped me off he said that if I ever told anyone, he'd kill my mother. I know I should have told someone, but I was too scared. I could have given the police information about Lirim, but I didn't know anything about Victor other than his first name. I was afraid that if the police arrested Lirim, Victor would have gone after me or my mother."

Sheriff Anbani asked her several more questions and Hannah answered them calmly. He assured her that he would personally make certain that her identity would not be revealed. "Thank you, Sheriff, I've been waiting for this day," she said. "I've never told a soul, and I don't know how I'll feel about it tomorrow, but it feels good to get it off of my conscience."

"I've been waiting fifteen years to find out the truth," Anbani said after ending the call. "I may have just put that young woman through hell, but I'm glad we finally have the real story."

"And I think Hannah will be better off, too," Gerry proffered. "I can't imagine how difficult it must have been for her to keep that secret bottled up for so many years."

"Agreed," Anbani replied. "Based on what we know, I'm pretty certain Hannah was the only victim. Lirim tried selling the photos in Morgantown, so he may not have had too many buyers on the carnival circuit."

"And within a few years, any clients he did have would have been able to find better quality images on the Internet," Damon said.

They continued to bat ideas around but collectively decided that Hannah was right. It was a money-making scheme made easy because Lirim knew Hannah's schedule. But it probably hadn't been a cash cow, and Lirim and Victor just moved on to their next venture.

Gerry Sloman had reserved a room at the same hotel as Damon, but needed to make phone calls to coordinate a transfer of Victor to West Virginia after he was arrested. Sheriff Anbani would work with his Marion County colleagues to determine which jurisdiction would handle the interrogation and prosecution on charges resulting from his conduct with Hannah Roscoph. But Gerry wanted the Arlington police to be involved in the interviews, too. His suspicion of Victor McElroy as a murderer had only risen.

Later that evening, Damon met Gerry in the hotel lobby. The Hampton Inn didn't have a bar and the men were too tired to venture outside, so they settled into comfortable lounge chairs in the open entryway. Save for a pair of receptionists who were out of earshot, they were alone.

Gerry had spoken with Margaret, who provided him with two significant pieces of information. The first was that the Front Royal police in western Virginia had picked up Victor McElroy. He was at home and gave up without resistance. The local police were searching his residence but hadn't uncovered any photographs, instant cameras or evidence that could tie him to Lirim's murder. Margaret was on her way to double check—the local police didn't have the same level of intimacy with the details of Lirim's murder.

Victor was being held in Front Royal and would be transferred to Morgantown in the morning. Gerry anticipated charges of accessory to kidnapping, child abuse and accessory to interstate distribution of child pornography.

The second piece of news was that the preliminary results of the autopsy were back. The medical examiner, Grace Chu, confirmed that Lirim had been the victim of two isolated strangulations. One set of marks was from a clothesline as they expected. The other set was from a bicycle chain.

The chain was rough and had done significant damage to the exterior of Lirim's throat. But based on the locations and angles of the marks, according to Grace Chu, it was the nylon clothesline that killed him. Coupled with medical evidence from the inner workings of Lirim's throat, Grace posited that not only had the clothesline killed Lirim, but it killed him prior to use of the chain. She couldn't say with any certainty how much time had passed between strangulations, but it had been a matter of hours rather than minutes.

"So that eliminates the theory that one person strangled him and left him unconscious and a second person came in later and finished the job," Gerry said in closing.

"And if hours passed between strangulations, it wasn't a murderer who started with one weapon, lost control of it and had to move to a second weapon," Damon said.

"Margaret and I think we're left with a single scenario, and Grace agrees. Lirim was strangled to death in his sleep with a clothesline. Hours later, a second person came in with the exact same intent, found Lirim in bed in the dark, thought he was asleep and choked him with a bicycle chain."

"Someone tried to kill a dead man," Damon said rhetorically. "It still seems pretty coincidental that two people would try to strangle the same man on the same night."

"I've been thinking about that. It could be explained if there was a recent event that triggered two people who each had a motive." Gerry sat forward in his chair. "As for method, I've been thinking about that too. In close proximity to the other trailers, a gunshot would make too much noise unless the killer had a silencer. So that would leave suffocation, strangulation and stabbing as the most likely means for murder. Suffocation would be too risky. Lirim was strong. Had he woken up and the murderer been armed with only a pillow, Lirim could have fought off the attacker. Of course that's possible with a strangulation too, but much less likely if the ligature is already around the person's neck."

"So that leaves knifing and strangulation."

"Exactly. And unlike with a knife, there's less risk of screaming with strangulation and no risk of getting blood on your clothes."

"Were any fingerprints found on the body?" Damon asked.

"No. And there was no blood or human tissue under Lirim's fingernails."

The men debated whether a prosecutor could pursue a charge for attempted murder after a man was already dead. Gerry was of the opinion that the county could.

Just before eleven, Damon and Gerry retired to their separate rooms. Gerry was meeting Margaret, Ravi Anbani and the Marion County sheriff early in the morning to discuss strategy for Victor's interrogation. Damon wasn't invited to join and resigned himself to driving home to Hollydale in the morning.

Chapter 16

Damon lay awake in the overnight hours beneath a thin blanket and stared at the light post outside of his hotel window. He turned over all of the facts of the case. There was a lot of information, and it was good information, but the pieces didn't all connect.

Tabby's death still troubled him. She died in a car accident less than two weeks after finding her husband's photos of an unclothed child. And it wasn't a straightforward accident. She had been driving in the middle of the night with no known objective. A large black vehicle struck Tabby's car head on. Did Lirim have one registered in his name or under Big Surf?

Three fourteen. Damon crawled out of the bed and composed an e-mail with his thoughts on vehicle registration to Gerry and Ravi Anbani. Damon woke four hours later and checked his phone. Ravi Anbani had responded with a simple, "Good thought, we'll look into it."

The journey home to Hollydale was uneventful as was his afternoon volunteering at the library. His thoughts turned to Bethany. Damon had secured good seats for Friday's musical at the Kennedy Center. The two days in West Virginia took his mind off of his upcoming date, but now, as the hours crawled by with no word from Gerry, trepidation over the pending evening with Bethany set in. He summoned his courage and called her to confirm a time to pick her up. To Damon's relief, Bethany didn't pick up and he left a message.

Gerry had promised to call and fill Damon in on the results of the police's interrogation of Victor, but Damon still hadn't heard from him when he left the library at five o'clock. He walked to The Cookery to see Rebecca. It was only a quarter of a mile, but he hadn't exercised in days so the walk felt good.

While Damon was in West Virginia, Hollydale had moved on from the murder in many ways. The fairgrounds were barren, the carnival caravan had driven off to its next destination and, as Margaret had informed Gerry the previous day, Jordan Hall and Clara Jovanović returned to Richmond and Toma had gone back to Baltimore.

Rebecca's shop smelled of fresh baked bread. She spooned a generous dollop of honey on an inch thick slice of sourdough and placed it on a napkin in front of him.

"Thanks," he said taking a sizeable bite and covering his open mouth with his hand. "This bread is phenomenal. It tastes like it took hours to make."

"Actually it takes four days," she said with a smile. She explained the fermentation process involved in a creating a multi-day sourdough starter—it sounded more like a dissertation defense than a baking instruction.

Rebecca brought a pitcher of pink lemonade and two pilsner glasses to the countertop and asked him what he had discovered about Anthony Weams. The anesthesiologist was all but a distant memory to Damon, but when he had breakfast with Rebecca less than three days earlier, Weams had been at the forefront of his suspicions. Damon filled her in with the details of his trip, but made sure to leave out Hannah Roscoph's name. The other fact he couldn't reveal to Rebecca was that there had been multiple strangulations. The police were still keeping that fact close to the vest.

After his morning shift at the library the following day, with still no message from Gerry, Damon decided to take a drive to Manassas, Virginia, where Big Surf was operating for the week. The area surrounding the Prince William County fair in Manassas was more spacious than the neighborhoods bordering the fairgrounds in Arlington, but within the boundaries of the fair itself the scenery was nearly identical.

The area housing the temporary living quarters was desolate. Damon remembered that Jim Riley had decided to move into Lirim's trailer. He wondered if the man had even bothered to buy a new mattress. The submarine style trailers all had similar features, but Damon recognized distinguishing characteristics—including the large metal initials "LJ"—on the one at the far end.

He approached the door and knocked. Jim invited Damon inside. The small table held a large accounting ledger. Bacon odor permeated stale air inside the trailer.

"I'm surprised to see you again," Jim said.

"I wanted to ask you a question about Lirim."

"Go ahead." Jim picked up the ledger and placed it in a cabinet beneath the small kitchen counter. "You're not the police, but I had nothing to do with Lirim's death so it doesn't bother me." Damon noticed the swelling on Jim's earlobe had diminished and the scrapes on his forearm were scabbed over.

"The Arlington police have been working with the sheriff's office in Morgantown, West Virginia," Damon started, leaving out his contribution.

"That's where Lirim lived."

Damon nodded. "About fifteen years ago, Lirim and Victor McElroy were involved in an illegal money making scheme."

"Sounds familiar," Jim said with a smirk.

"But it was much worse. Lirim and Victor kidnapped an eleven-year-old girl, took illicit photos of her and sold copies of them."

Jim balled his fists. "What a couple of sickos." His indignation seemed genuine.

"My thoughts exactly," Damon said.

"So did the girl come back and choke the life out of Lirim?"

"I don't think so," Damon replied. His brain wrinkled. He, Gerry and Ravi Anbani had accepted Hannah Roscoph's word that she hadn't told anyone about Lirim and Victor. But if she had lied, there could be an entire set of suspects to Lirim's murder unknown to the police. And for that matter, the call to Hannah took place five days after the murder—she could have killed him herself.

"Well, if you don't think she killed Lirim, what does it have to do with me?" Jim asked, interrupting Damon's thoughts.

"I wanted to know whether he and Victor were still in the business."

"You mean were they stripping down little kids in this very trailer and taking pictures?"

"Either that or selling copies of pictures he already had to anyone on the carnival circuit."

The smaller man looked Damon straight in the eyes. "I can't be positive. I wasn't watching him all of the time, but I don't think he was doing anything like that. At least not for the past five years when I was his partner."

"And distribution?"

"I doubt it. Not everyone in the carnival game is as clean as a whistle, but I just didn't see anything of that sort."

"Well, he had photos fifteen years ago and the police believe he sold them while he traveled with Big Surf."

"Fifteen years was a long time ago, before every joker had a wireless tablet or access to a laptop," Jim said. "But it wasn't Big Surf back then."

Damon raised his eyebrows with interest.

"Lirim called it Mountaineer Carnivals," Jim continued. "When I invested, he shut down that corporation and started Big Surf to make the legalities easier."

Damon wondered whether Gerry knew about the corporate change. And if a black SUV could be registered to a corporation, could it have been registered to Mountaineer Carnivals?

Jim was being helpful, but there was still one piece of information Damon wanted from him. He decided to jump in feet first and hoped he wouldn't regret it. No one knew he was in Jim's trailer, or even in Manassas.

"Jim, you said you're not afraid to talk, but you are hiding something, aren't you?"

Jim's narrow face twitched and he sat down on the worn pea-green sofa. "I don't know what you're talking about," he said flatly.

"There's a reason you didn't file a civil suit against Lirim and Victor to reclaim your share of the money Big Surf paid the IRS. The same reason, I'm guessing, you didn't go back to the IRS or to the police when you found out they starting skimming again."

"The IRS penalized the company the first time. Why would I want to bring them back?" He conjured as much bravado as he could muster.

"Because they weren't just skimming tax dollars, but profits as well. Profits that you were entitled to your fair share of. And the IRS has a criminal investigation arm. They may not have been called in the first time, but you could have been pretty certain they would have been involved if the IRS found out Lirim and Victor had started skimming again."

Riley scratched his chin with vigor. "I know, I know," he said. "The reason I kept my mouth closed has nothing to do with Lirim's death, but I just can't tell you what it is." His eyes took on an oily quality.

"If you don't come clean, the police may arrest you for murder," Damon said. It wasn't technically a lie.

But Jim picked up on the nuance. "The police *may* arrest me?"

"I don't know whether they will or not, but look at it from their point of view," Damon said. "With Lirim dead, the skimming stops immediately. You get to fire Victor and you can buy out Lirim's share of Big Surf from Clara. Everyone in town seems to know about the clothesline used to strangle Lirim, and you knew where it was kept. You have some pretty nasty looking scratches on your forearm that didn't appear until just after the murder. And on top of all of that, there's a secret reason you can't tattle on your business partner and his henchman accountant. If you were the police and your other leads had run cold, what would you do?"

Jim Riley grunted. He stood up from the sofa, retrieved a can of root beer from the refrigerator and contemplated the nutrition label.

"It's pretty simple really," he said a full minute later, still staring at the soda. "When I was getting ready to buy into Big Surf, I needed a loan—basically a mortgage on my half of the company. I had a decent amount of money saved, but nowhere near enough for a full share. I didn't own my home and had no other collateral. I applied for a business loan with two banks but they both turned me down, so I went to Lirim and told him the deal was off. I couldn't get the financing."

Damon nodded his head.

"Lirim got very upset," Jim continued. "This was right around the time when he was involved with the Florida venture capitalists. I'm pretty sure he needed cash, and quickly. Lirim had already mortgaged most of the carnival's equipment and couldn't get another loan himself."

Damon's mind jumped to the Florida venture capitalists. He had forgotten about them, though he was sure Gerry hadn't. "So what were you buying into?" Damon asked.

"Contracts and goodwill with the counties, mainly. Lirim had an established relationship with a number of fairs and that's like platinum in the carnival business. Also, he had the infrastructure all set up, employees and equipment."

"Okay, I get it. Lirim needed an infusion of money and couldn't get it himself. He had you lined up—a buyer with a cash down payment but in need of a loan for the remainder."

"Right. So when I told Lirim I was pulling out—after he initially blew up, he calmed down and told me not to worry. Two days later, he set up a meeting for me with a man who called himself China." He picked at the scab on his arm. "China wasn't Chinese—he looked Russian or maybe Ukrainian. He was basically a rogue financial advisor. He helped me create a fraudulent account, which made it look like I had a large investment portfolio that could be collateralized. And he knew a small business loan manager who, for a percentage of the loan value, would look the other way if the paperwork was reasonable on its face. Unlike Lirim, I didn't have any other mortgages, so it didn't raise any red flags at the upper levels of the bank." Jim Riley dropped his head into his hands. "If I told anyone about the skimming, Lirim would have exposed me."

"You don't know China's real name?" Damon asked.

"I honestly don't, and I don't know where to find him," Jim said. "Everything was done under my name. I can probably dig up the name of the loan manager. I'm sure the police will ask for it."

Damon told Jim that he appreciated his candor.

"Do you think the police will arrest me for fraud?" Jim asked.

"I don't know," Damon said. The staleness in the trailer was starting to constrict his throat and sitting less than fifteen feet from where a dead body had lain didn't help.

Damon exited the trailer, leaving a despondent-looking Jim lying on the sofa. Damon bent over and took several deep breaths of fresh air. It cleared his throat, and he strolled briskly through the fairgrounds back to his car.

He wondered what would happen to the arrangement Skipper had with Jim to pay for his schooling if Jim was incarcerated. Could the argument he witnessed between Skipper and Lirim have been about something more significant than a week's pay? If Lirim was threatening to expose Jim Riley's fraud and Skipper knew about it, Skipper's tuition money would dry up.

Damon checked himself. Lirim had no reason to expose Jim's fraud. Otherwise, he would be an accomplice for setting up the arrangement. Then again, Lirim had apparently used the threat of exposure to keep Jim from halting the skimming scheme.

Before starting his vehicle, Damon called Gerry Sloman to inform him of Jim's confession. Gerry answered on the second ring.

"Gerry. I haven't heard from you in almost two days. What's happening?"

"A lot, Damon. I'm driving back to Arlington as we speak."

"I just spoke the Jim Riley," Damon said. "I figured out what he's been hiding."

"Damn it, Damon, you can't just approach a suspect on your own. Listen, come over for dinner tonight and fill me in."

Chapter 17

Damon arrived at Gerry and Trina Sloman's house bearing a bottle of red table wine. He knew Gerry wouldn't partake of more than a minimal amount while he was in the throes of a major case, but Trina would appreciate the gesture. She invited him into the stone-fronted house and Gerry greeted Damon with a fatigued handshake.

They ate homemade lasagna and a terrific salad in the Sloman's well-appointed dining room. Trina provided a defensive "we rarely have guests," even though neither man had challenged the formal location. The conversation over the meal was light, and Trina was interested in Damon's upcoming evening with Bethany, who hadn't yet returned his call.

After coffee, Trina retreated from the dining room and left Gerry and Damon to discuss the case. Gerry asked Damon to provide details of his conversation with Jim Riley, and after Damon was finished Gerry requested that he refrain from interviewing any other suspects. "Margaret is worried that you're too involved," Gerry said. "Listen, I appreciate using you as a sounding board, but you're being too proactive. And approaching a suspect on your own was downright dangerous."

Gerry would pass along Jim's bank fraud story to the police's financial crime unit. Damon asked if the police had made any progress in tracking down Lirim's venture capitalist contacts in Florida.

"There were some phone numbers Anbani's deputies found in a file cabinet in Lirim's West Virginia home," Gerry said. "But they were all linked to pre-paid cell phones registered under phony names."

"Will you have Sheriff Anbani check into Mountaineer Carnivals for registration of a black vehicle?" Damon asked, filling his coffee cup from a cordless percolator.

"No need," replied Gerry. His cheeks flushed—he had good news to relay and wanted to relish the moment. "Victor McElroy owned a black SUV and he says Lirim used it to murder his wife."

Damon took in the information and watched Gerry watching him. "Very convenient that a dead man murdered Tabby," Damon said.

"Agreed. But now Anbani has officially moved Tabby's death from an accident to a suspicious death. I'll get to that part, but let me start at the beginning."

Trina came in with a plate of store-bought lemon pastries, set it between the men, who were seated across the table from each other, and withdrew wordlessly.

"On Tuesday morning, the Front Royal police delivered Victor to the sheriff's station in Morgantown," Gerry said. "The Fairmont sheriff's office is under construction and given our background on the case, Anbani and I were handling the interrogation while Margaret and the Fairmont sheriff listened in. Victor declined legal representation." Gerry bit into a pastry and licked crumbs from his fingers. "We started by setting the photocopies of Hannah Roscoph on the table in front of him. Victor denied ever seeing them. So we played the recording we made of Hannah, which pointed to Victor as the photographer. We pushed him hard, insisting that we'd be going after full kidnapping and distribution of child pornography charges if he didn't admit to snapping the photos."

"I bet he was sweating when he heard the tape."

"That's an understatement. After almost an hour, Victor admitted to taking the pictures, but said that he had been victimized by Lirim. He said it was Lirim who kidnapped the girl and made the sales. He took the Polaroids but only because Lirim threatened to kill him if he didn't participate."

"Do you believe that?" Damon asked.

"I believe Lirim brought the girl to the mobile home by himself because that's what Hannah said. As for who made the sales, we'll see how many customers we can find. And Anbani will interview the men who approached Sheriff Greely fifteen years ago if he can identify them. But Victor said sales were almost non-existent—according to Lirim, that is. He said the only people he knew who bought photocopies from Lirim were a vendor who sold carnival prizes in bulk and a maintenance worker at one of the community centers that doubled as a fairground."

"And Sheriff Greely?"

"Victor said he had no idea. We didn't want to press him and have him change his mind on a lawyer, so we let it go for now."

"What about other girls?"

"Victor insisted there were no others. It was a one-time incident. Lirim had heard the carnival prize vendor talking about how it was nearly impossible to get his hands on materials of that type, and Lirim saw it as a potential stream of revenue. He knew of an eleven-year-old girl, and he had at least one potential buyer. My guess is that between a lack of buyers and the significant risk, Lirim moved on after Hannah Roscoph."

"Especially after the Morgantown locals went to the sheriff."

"Exactly. Lirim probably thought he was the luckiest person on Earth when he convinced the sheriff to look the other way. I suspect we'll never know if the sheriff wanted photos in exchange for his silence or if Lirim had some dirt on him. Greely passed away several years ago."

"The sickest part about all of this," Damon replied, "is that Lirim had a daughter almost the same age as Hannah."

"Agreed," said Gerry. "But for Lirim, I don't think that photographing Hannah was anything other than a means to an end. No different than finding Jim Riley a crooked accountant."

"Then why would he keep the originals and a couple of sets of copies?"

"He may have thought the threat of exposing the photos publicly would thwart Hannah if he ever found out she intended to tell the police."

Damon looked into his coffee cup, then stood and reached to the end of the table where Trina had thoughtfully left his wine glass and the bottle of table wine. He poured himself a generous portion. It was only his second glass of the night.

"Tell me about Victor's black SUV," Damon said and sat back down.

Trina had also left out a clear glass pitcher of water that resembled the classic shape of the Kool-Aid man. Gerry poured himself a tall glass. Damon reflected on how fortunate Gerry was to have Trina and found himself craving a similar comfort.

"Ravi Anbani's deputies found two vehicles registered to Victor McElroy, both in Virginia. He has an old Chevy Caprice and a ten-year-old black Chevy Tahoe."

"A Tahoe is pretty large, isn't it?" Damon asked.

"It is, my friend. We also checked all of Lirim's vehicles, both under his own name and that of Big Surf. He has a fleet, including all of the mobile homes and hauling trailers. One that didn't garner our attention initially is a flatbed tow truck. But according to Victor, Lirim murdered his wife and then used both Victor's Tahoe and the flatbed to arrange a bogus accident scene."

"And Victor was nowhere in the vicinity, I assume," Damon said facetiously.

"That's what he said, but I don't buy it. Either way, we pounded the basics of his story out of him. He thinks it will get him leniency on the child abuse charges that he knows are coming."

"Will it?"

"I doubt it, but that's for the prosecutors in West Virginia to decide."

"I'm still surprised he admitted that his truck was involved in killing Tabby."

"He thought about it a good long time before he admitted to it. Margaret had stepped into the interview room, jabbed a finger in Victor's face and told him the police were running the paint on Victor's SUV against black paint recovered a year and a half ago from Tabby's crushed Cavalier. Our lab techs do match paint samples, but there's no way Anbani still has the Cavalier in his impound lot given that it was ruled an accident. But the threat was enough to squirrel a story out of Victor."

Gerry dipped a thumb and forefinger into his water glass, removed a lemon slice and sucked it between his teeth. "Victor said that a few days before Tabby died, he and Lirim went to Roanoke to look at some equipment being sold off piecemeal by a carnival operator retiring from the business. It was off season so they drove separately from their respective homes.

Lirim took a sedan and Victor drove the black Tahoe. They purchased some equipment that would fit in the Tahoe but not the sedan. Lirim wanted to refurbish it, so Victor says they exchanged vehicles. They planned to swap the vehicles back a couple of weeks later when they had another trip scheduled."

"Why would Lirim take a sedan to buy equipment that didn't fit in it?" Damon asked.

"I have no idea and neither did Victor. Anbani asked him that exact question."

Damon nodded. "So according to Victor, he wasn't in Morgantown when Tabby died, but his SUV was."

"That's his story."

"But if Victor wasn't in Morgantown, how does he know she wasn't killed in a car accident?"

"He said Lirim told him the truth because when they re-swapped vehicles, the front end of the Tahoe was smashed."

Gerry twisted the gold cross at the end of his thin necklace and continued. "According to Victor, Lirim told him that Tabby found a stash of photos of Hannah Roscoph. Tabby didn't want to turn him in to the police but planned to remove Lirim as an after-death beneficiary of her trust principal. Lirim confided to Victor that he couldn't get a proper read on Tabby. He didn't know if she'd follow through on her threat to change her will or if she'd change her mind and inform the police. For Lirim, killing his wife would solve both problems."

"She obviously didn't rush to change the will if she died almost two weeks after she found the photos," Damon said.

"I bet Lirim was watching her like a hawk. But still, if Lirim met Victor in Roanoke just before she died, Tabby would have had at least a day on her own to consult with a lawyer."

Gerry poured another glass of water for himself. Damon continued to take tiny sips of the wine already in his glass. "When Lirim told Victor he killed Tabby, he supplied plenty of detail," Gerry said. "Tabby didn't sneak out for a late night drive—Lirim killed her right in their house. While she was sleeping, he smothered her with a pillow. Lirim either looked up asphyxiation online or got lucky. Smothering leaves only minor external indicators, so as long as the police at the accident scene didn't call in a medical examiner, they wouldn't be able to tell how she really died."

"So Lirim faked an accident to cover murdering Tabby in their own bed," Damon said.

"That's the story we were told. Lirim drove Tabby's Cavalier around the back of the house in Cheat Lake and left the engine running so the airbag would deploy. Then he put her dead body in the front seat and left off her seat belt. That would make her death by car crash more believable." Gerry was tugging hard now at the cross around his neck. "Lirim climbed into Victor's black Tahoe and drove as fast as he could into the Cavalier, causing the airbag to explode into Tabby's lifeless face."

"It must have given Lirim a pretty big jolt."

"I'm sure it did. Lirim's back yard is almost a full acre of packed dirt so he could have gotten going pretty fast. After crushing the Cavalier, Lirim hoisted it onto the flatbed and drove it to the road where Simon Chenter found it on his way to work a few hours later."

"Pretty big risk if he was seen in the tow truck."

"Maybe not," Gerry said. "It was well past midnight and on rural back roads. Lirim probably threw a blanket over the body. Also, those flatbed style tow trucks are raised high off the ground so her body wouldn't have been at eye-level to a car passing in the other direction."

Damon thought for a minute. He put the wine glass to his lips but set it back down without drinking. "I'm trying to figure out Victor's motives. Why provide you with so much detail?"

"My guess is that he didn't plan on saying anything. But once Victor felt cornered into admitting that his SUV was on the scene because of the paint, I think he wanted to dictate a clean story that he could control. That way, even if we could link his truck to the incident, the only person who could refute his account is Lirim. And he's dead."

"Okay, but I still see one main problem with Victor's story," Damon said. "Why would Lirim go through all of the trouble to get Victor's Tahoe to Morgantown but then turn around and tell Victor he used it to kill Tabby? If Lirim didn't want to use one of his own vehicles, that makes sense. And maybe he wanted to use Victor's SUV in case he needed to blackmail Victor later."

"Or frame him," Gerry interjected.

"Right. Either way, I can see why he wanted Victor's truck. But why would Lirim proceed to tell Victor what he had done and with that level of detail? Why not just fix the truck himself? He was able to fix all of his carnival equipment."

"We're on the same page, Damon. That's exactly why Margaret and I think Victor was in Morgantown with Lirim when Tabby was killed. Even if he didn't have the right parts to do the bodywork, Lirim could have just told Victor that he was in an accident himself."

"Exactly," Damon said. "I'd be shocked if Victor wasn't involved. He was involved with Hannah Roscoph even though Lirim could have handled that scheme by himself."

Gerry nodded his agreement.

"And Lirim's killer?" Damon asked.

"We know a whole lot more about Lirim's back story, but that's all so far."

"I'd be surprised if there wasn't a connection."

"Me too. It's just a matter of finding it. I'm going to cull through all of my notes and documents and see if there's something I'm missing. I grilled Victor about Lirim's death again but couldn't find out anything we didn't already know."

Damon wished Gerry good luck with his files and left him to recover from his arduous but fruitful two days in Morgantown.

Chapter 18

David Einstaff was on their shared front porch when Damon arrived home. It was fairly late, even for David to be out.

Damon greeted him pleasantly. "How are you, David?"

The older man had been staring at his shoes and looked up. Even before he spoke, Damon could see that David had consumed more than his typical evening allotment of whiskey. "Damon, I'm not doing too well to be honest with you."

Damon sat in the green plastic patio chair beside David and asked him what was wrong.

"I think I'm sinking into a mild depression, Damon. I'm having trouble finding pleasure in life right now."

He picked up a fresh cigarette and brought it to his lips by force of habit but remembered his company and set it down again. Damon waited for him to continue. "I had a reasonably happy life—a wife, three kids and a couple of cats in the suburbs. I'm a wastewater engineer at a small firm here in Arlington. Not exciting, but I've done solid work for thirty years. After the last of my kids went to college, my wife and I started nitpicking each other over simple things. Things that each of us had already been doing for years, but all of a sudden, rather than overlook them, we castigated each other. Our divorce became final three weeks ago."

Damon put a hand on his neighbor's shoulder. David had only shared the duplex with him for four months, but Damon assumed he'd been divorced the entire time.

"One night next week, we'll go out for a guys' night," Damon said. "If Gerry Sloman's finished with the case he's working on, I'll invite him. And Teddy Fitzroy who lives a few blocks away. He manages the bowling alley in South Arlington—he's single and is always up for some fun. We'll go to dinner at a steakhouse and then hit one of the live music lounges down in Clarendon. What do you say?"

David looked at him appreciatively. "You really don't have to do all of that, Damon."

"I need a night like that myself, David. Consider it done." Damon rose to his feet. "I'll set it up and let you know what night works for everyone."

David returned his hand to his tumbler and raised his drink. "Thanks, Damon. You know what Henny Youngman said? 'When I read about the evils of drinking, I gave up reading.'"

"Just don't overdo it, David."

Standing behind the library's front desk the following day, Damon thought about his trip to Morgantown. Johnnetta Frank hadn't told him everything she knew, he felt certain, and it was gnawing at him. He replayed their conversation in his mind. It was when he asked whether she had told anyone Tabby found the photos of Hannah Roscoph that Johnnetta lied. So who did she tell?

Damon arrived home shortly after five in the afternoon. The message light was blinking and Damon instinctively knew it was Bethany. He hit play and heard her voice. "Damon, it's Bethany Krims. I'm sorry I didn't call you back earlier. Listen, tomorrow night isn't going to work for me. Thank you very much for the invitation. I'm sure I'll see you around."

Click.

Damon winced. In the back of his mind he had expected it, but hearing her words still stung. Bethany hadn't said she "couldn't" make it but that "it wasn't going to work." There was a big difference. She hadn't cancelled because something came up to prevent her from joining him. Rather, she changed her mind and decided to cut him off at the knees.

He called his mother and offered her the tickets to the show at the Kennedy Center. She accepted and had the good grace not to question what happened with Bethany. She would ask in a few days, but not while the wound was still fresh.

"Will you take Charles Swickley?" Damon asked.

"I don't think so, Damon. Charles is a nice man and I've enjoyed spending time with him, but I'm not going to let it get serious. He's far too old for me."

Damon was pleased Lynne Lassard-Brown had finally come to this realization.

"Would you consider taking David Einstaff?" he asked.

"No, I thought I'd ask Rebecca. I like that girl and think it would be nice for me to get to know her even better."

Even though she hadn't come out and asked whether Bethany had broken off the Friday night engagement, his mother must have sensed as much. And she was making another salvo in Rebecca's favor. Perhaps he was the only one who failed to appreciate that Rebecca was the right woman for him.

Damon found an online directory listing and dialed Johnnetta Frank. He wrestled with his conscience and justified the call—Johnnetta Frank wasn't a suspect. The telephone rang nine times before she answered.

"Hello?" came the familiar timid voice through the receiver.

"Hello Mrs. Frank. This is Damon Lassard. We met on Monday. I came to your house just before the sheriff did."

"I certainly remember you, Mr. Lassard. One doesn't forget the person to whom she tells her secrets."

That's an opening, Damon thought. He took a breath. "A secret is why I'm calling Mrs. Frank. Two secrets actually. One that I know about, and one that I believe you have."

He heard quiet sounds on the other end of the line. Damon pictured Johnnetta Frank crossing her arms in front of her chest and rubbing her shoulders to warm them.

"The secret I know about," Damon said, "is that Lirim Jovanović didn't act alone when he took those pictures." He summarized Victor's role in the conspiracy and told her they found the girl in the pictures, but he didn't disclose Hannah's name.

"Is she well now?"

"She is, Mrs. Frank. She's twenty-five years old and lives in California. I think that Lirim's death and the arrest of Victor McElroy will give her the closure she needs."

"Thank goodness," she said quietly.

"Mrs. Frank. I've given you a lot of information because I feel you have the right to know. You've been carrying a burden for the past year and a half and I hope this news helps you."

"It does. Thank you, Mr. Lassard. And now you want more from me. Is that right?"

The pair had not bartered ahead of time, but Johnnetta Frank recognized the debt owed for Damon's generosity. "That's right, ma'am." Damon chose his next words carefully. He didn't want to accuse her of lying. "Mrs. Frank, I think there may be something that you've remembered since we spoke. Someone you told about the pictures Tabby found."

"Yes," she replied meekly, but without hesitation. "It's about time I came out with it. I did tell someone. It was eating away at me. Less than two weeks after Tabby found those pictures and she dies. It was just too big of a coincidence, and Tabby would never drive anywhere in the middle of the night. I tried to convince myself that she and Lirim must have had a fight and she raced out of the house to escape. That she was so frantic she forget to put on her seat belt. But if they had a bad argument, Tabby would have come to my house. Lirim would have known to try here first if Tabby left him, but he never came looking for her. No, I just don't think she was running, which is why I've been suspicious about her death, and Lirim in particular."

"Why didn't you express your concerns to the sheriff's office?"

"They wouldn't have believed the ramblings of an old woman, and I just couldn't bring myself to get involved. It wouldn't have brought Tabby back."

Damon decided against telling Johnnetta that if Victor was to be believed, her suspicions were dead on and Lirim had in fact killed Tabby.

"I understand," Damon said even though he didn't. "Please go on."

"It's silly. About three weeks ago I was watching a made-for-television movie late at night. It was about a man who killed his wife and tried to cover it up. I started crying. I had tried so hard to put Tabby and her accident out of my mind, but this movie brought all of my emotions and suspicions back. I needed to talk about it with someone." Her voice broke. She was on the verge of tears. "I like the sheriff, but I wanted to talk to a woman. And I wanted to tell the one person I should have told at the outset. Clara Jovanović."

"You told Clara three weeks ago about Tabby finding the pictures?"

"I did. And that it happened just before her car accident. Clara and Tabby were close, especially when Clara was young. I felt she should know the truth about her father and my concerns about her mother's death."

"Did you go to see her or speak over the telephone?"

"She came to see me. Tabby had given me Clara's cellular number several years ago. Tabby hadn't been well—too much smoking. So she gave me Lirim's and Clara's numbers in case anything happened to her. I called Clara and told her I had some news about her parents and asked her to come see me. I told her it was serious and I would only feel comfortable discussing it in person. She was able to move some shifts around at her hospital and come here two days later."

"And you told her everything you know?"

"Yes, I told her exactly the same thing I told you."

"Thank you, Mrs. Frank," Damon said. "How did she react?"

"She looked beaten down. Not angry, just sad. She thanked me politely and drove away." Johnnetta coughed gently. "Please tell me Clara didn't kill her father. Not that the son of a you-know-what didn't deserve it, but I couldn't stand to see Clara go to prison."

"I don't know if she killed him. I hope she didn't," Damon said with empathy and thanked Johnnetta Frank for her time.

Chapter 19

Johnnetta Frank told Clara that her father had tried his hand in the child pornography business. In addition, given the timing of Tabby's discovery of the photos, Johnnetta suspected Lirim played a role in his wife's death. And that, Damon thought, is why Johnnetta didn't initially divulge that she had spoken with Clara—she was afraid that Clara murdered her father.

Clara had been with Anthony Weams on the night of the murder. She and Anthony could have done it together. Or for that matter, Clara, Anthony and Jordan Hall could all have been in on it. The double affair proffered to the police by the three, Clara cheating on Jordan and Anthony on his wife, could be an elaborate cover up.

Damon looked at the clock. It was just after six thirty in the evening. Richmond was a little more than one hundred miles south of Hollydale, but in Thursday evening rush hour traffic, the drive would take at least two hours. He grabbed a soda from the kitchen and sped off in the Saab to Virginia's state capital. Damon didn't have Clara's home address but he remembered the name of the hospital where she worked—St. Michael's.

Between a crude navigation system on his phone and a helpful clerk at a gas station, Damon located the hospital. It was old and decaying, probably not unlike many of its patients. There were multiple parking lots and he avoided the one nearest the emergency room.

Damon didn't want to encounter Jordan Hall before he could speak with Clara.

He approached the front desk at the main hospital entrance and asked for the geriatric medicine unit. The receptionist pointed to an elevator bank and directed him to the west wing of the fourth floor.

The ward's lobby was a small oval with a series of hallways sprouting in every direction, not dissimilar to a spider. He told the on-duty nurse he was a friend of Clara's, giving her the impression that Clara was expecting to see him. Damon was in luck— she was on shift, although it didn't end for another hour.

Damon killed time in the cafeteria, trying not to think about the fat content in the mayonnaise binding his egg-salad sandwich. He debated calling Gerry Sloman. He would need to tell the detective about Johnnetta's disclosure soon, but if he called now, Gerry would insist that he not speak to Clara. He convinced himself that meeting her wasn't an interview, just a conversation with a relatively new friend. And he'd call Gerry right after he spoke with Clara.

At ten minutes before the end of Clara's shift, Damon made his way back to the geriatric wing. As he began to lower himself into a stuffed brown chair, Clara strode confidently into the lobby and met Damon's gaze. Damon hadn't fantasized about Clara in a short white nurse's dress, so her baby-blue uniform jacket and gray scrub pants didn't surprise him. Her thick dark hair had a lustrous sheen and was pulled back into a short pony tail. Her face looked as if she had just scrubbed it with soap.

"Hi Damon," she said sweetly. "I didn't expect to see you again."

"Hi Clara. I'd like to talk to you about something. Are you done here for the night?"

"I am. I'm pretty tired, but there's a coffee shop around the corner if you want to buy me a cup." She squeezed his forearm with a trembling hand and said she'd be back in a minute after she signed off on her patients' charts.

Damon waited for five minutes before anxiety set in. Was there another exit she had taken to escape? No, he thought, that would just make her look guilty. And two minutes later, she appeared and apologized for the delay. Damon chided himself. Clara had been nothing but nice—more than nice— to him.

Zorbi's coffee shop was nestled between a discount auto parts dealer and a vacuum supply store along a cracked sidewalk. Amateurish painted fireworks adorned the windows. The inside was dimly lit and Damon's chair felt grimy but the place was deserted. Clara had correctly surmised that this conversation warranted privacy above all else.

They reviewed plastic coated menus, but when the waitress arrived each settled for black coffee.

Clara pulled the band from her hair and let it out. Thick tufts splayed wildly after being confined for an entire day. "So Damon, what's so important that you need to speak with me in person after ten o'clock in Richmond?" The sweet smile had been replaced with cool skepticism.

"There's something about your father I'd like to discuss with you," he replied.

"If it's about his estate, yes, I'm entitled to it, and I think you know that. There's not much there other than a mortgaged interest in the carnival, which I'm selling to Jim Riley."

"And the house in Morgantown," Damon added. He didn't point out that Lirim's death cleared the way for Clara to recover a large sum from Tabby's estate. Her one third share and anything that was left from Lirim's share.

"Yes, that dump in Morgantown, too. I may have grown up there, but my father let the place waste away after Mom died. I wouldn't be surprised if it was overrun with rats and insects, the way he used to leave food out."

Damon leaned forward. "But you've been there recently and know that it is infested, don't you?"

The waitress appeared with a pair of glazed ceramic mugs.

Clara dropped her gaze and blew gently over the top of her coffee. Her head still bowed, she said, "Tell me what you want to know, Damon."

Damon took a sip of the scalding hot java, retracted his frame and slouched down. "Your old neighbor, Johnnetta Frank, told me that you went to see her. I know about your father's photographs and that your mother found them less than two weeks before her death."

Clara's expression saddened into puppy-dog eyes. Damon wanted to cross the table and hold her in his arms.

"Yes," she said softly. "Johnnetta told me. That was less than a week before I met you at the Fish Barrel." She paused. "I heard rumors when I was in tenth grade about a local man selling dirty pictures of a little girl, but I never knew it was my father. The sheriff must have searched our house while I was at school."

Damon told her the police believed Lirim was motivated solely by money and that Victor McElroy was involved. He left out the part about Lirim cheating on Tabby with Hannah Roscoph's mother.

"Did they lock up that asshole Victor?" she asked.

"Yes, he's being held in West Virginia."

"Good. Was Victor there when my father killed my mom, too?"

"I don't know." He stopped. "Clara, do you know for certain that Lirim killed your mother?"

Clara sipped her coffee for several seconds. "Just based on what Johnnetta said and what I know about my father's temperament."

"Did you discuss it with him?"

She glanced toward the café's door and then directed her attention back to Damon. "I did. Along with Toma."

Damon let the information sink in. Not only did Clara believe that Lirim killed her mother, but Toma probably believed that Lirim killed his sister.

She continued. "On the morning of the day you saw us at the Fish Barrel, I asked Toma to meet me in Arlington. He came down from Baltimore and I drove up from Richmond. I told him about the pictures and that Mom confronted my father just before her accident. Toma and I decided that my father must have killed her. There's no way he would risk her going to the police or cutting him out of her will."

Damon recalled meeting Toma at breakfast with Clara three days later. He had sneered when the topic of Tabby's death arose, as if he didn't believe it had been an accident. Now Damon knew why. "And the two of you went to see Lirim?"

"Yes, in the early afternoon. We met on the elementary school playground right next to the fairgrounds. It was far enough away not to be noticed by the carnival workers."

"What did you say to Lirim?"

"I didn't say anything. My father didn't say much, either. Toma pushed him a couple of times and flat out accused him of killing my mom. My father denied it, of course. Toma said he didn't care about the pictures of the little girl, though it thoroughly disgusted me."

"Did Toma threaten to kill him?" Damon asked frankly.

Clara didn't answer and the silence was telling.

"So that's why you haven't told the police any of this?" he asked, not expecting an answer. "You think Toma killed your father and you're protecting him. Or do you know that Toma killed him?" Toma as the murderer made sense.

"I have no idea if Toma killed my father," Clara said, her voice raised. Then, trying to deflect the line of inquiry, she said softly, "Lirim asked how we knew about the photos."

"Did you tell him?"

"No. I was afraid for Johnnetta Frank's safety. I didn't want my father going after her, though he probably suspected her. Mom didn't have many friends."

"Did Lirim happen to mention whether Victor was in Morgantown when Tabby was killed?" Damon asked.

"No, he didn't say a word about Victor. But I think Victor overheard the entire conversation. Or at least saw it."

"At the playground?"

"Yes. We were standing near a jungle gym, which is near the edge of the playground, where it backs up against the woodlands.""And you saw Victor there?"

"I think so. My father's back was to the woods and Toma and I were facing him, so I don't think my father knew he was there. But Victor probably followed him, in parallel through the woods. At one point, when Toma got up close to my father's face, I pushed my way in between them and noticed movement from the woods. It was a bright afternoon and I'm fairly certain I saw a human figure and that it was Victor."

"Your father selected the location next to the jungle gym?"

"He suggested we meet at the playground, and when we arrived he was there waiting for us."

"So Lirim and Victor could have set up the location ahead of time, just in case it got rough."

Clara looked Damon directly in the eyes. Her smoldering sensuality had returned. "I hadn't thought of that, Damon. You're very intelligent."

"Not really," Damon said modestly.

"I'm surprised Victor hasn't told the police yet. He must be keeping what he saw between Toma and my father in his back pocket to plea bargain."

That explained why Clara decided to come clean now about her and Toma confronting Lirim the day before he was killed. Now that Victor was behind bars, the confrontation was bound to surface anyway —the information was a strike against Toma and when the moment was right, Victor would play that card.

Damon said, "The night I saw you in the Fish Barrel, you were having dinner with Jordan when Lirim and Victor joined you. It seemed to me that you were expecting them."

"That was Jordan's doing. I was able to convince Toma to leave my father at the playground. No good was going to result from the encounter. After Toma and I parted, I called Jordan and let him know I was in Arlington. I made the excuse that I was here visiting a friend, but that I heard that Big Surf was handling the fair. It gave me an excuse to vent my frustrations against my father." She licked her lips. "I didn't tell Jordan anything, but he knew I was upset about the money from my Mom's estate. He insisted on coming to Arlington to discuss the matter with my father."

"So when you met at the Fish Barrel, no one mentioned the encounter at the playground only a few hours earlier?"

"No," Clara replied, reaching across the table and stroking the back of Damon's hand lightly with her fingertips. "It didn't make sense for me to raise it in front of Jordan, and I'm certain my father didn't want to notify him."

Damon didn't retract his hand and allowed Clara to pick it up and press it between both of hers. It was an intimate gesture and Damon's feelings shifted from pity to lust to nervousness that Clara could be manipulating him. She knew every word she uttered would go straight to the Arlington police.

The waitress refilled their mugs, and Damon wondered whether he'd see Clara again. The police would bring her in for more questioning. And then she would either be arrested or come back to Richmond and continue her life here. Hollydale was less than two hours away, but she would probably want to sever all ties to the ugliness that had fallen on her life in the past several weeks.

It was after midnight when Damon started the drive north back to Arlington. He plugged in a hands-free telephone device and called Gerry. It was late, but Damon knew he had crossed a boundary by driving to Richmond to speak with Clara on his own. He didn't want to exacerbate his transgression by sitting on the information he had gleaned.

An exhausted sounding Gerry answered. Damon reported the details of his conversations with Johnnetta Frank and Clara Jovanović.

"You have to be kidding me," Gerry lashed. "You may have just cost us the opportunity to catch a murderer."

Damon was stunned. "What do you mean?"

"I mean that you butted in one too many times, Damon. The police would have handled the information from Johnnetta Frank a lot differently. By speaking with Clara and driving away, she'll give Toma the chance to run."

"But running would only make him look guilty."

"He probably is guilty," Gerry responded with fury. "He just found out that his brother-in-law may have killed his sister, he confronted Lirim the day before the murder and he doesn't have an alibi for the night of the strangling itself."

The last part was news to Damon. "What did he say he was doing last Wednesday night?"

"Hold on, Damon. Let me make a couple of calls to see if the Baltimore police can track down Toma. You really stepped over the line this time."

Ten minutes passed in silence as Damon sped up I-95 in the direction of the nation's capital. His head ached with guilt. Damon knew deep down he shouldn't have been so proactive. His justifications had been mired in selfishness. After all, he had no experience and no training in detective work.

Damon didn't expect a call back, but Gerry was a faithful friend no matter how upset he was at Damon. The detective called and continued the conversation as if there had been no pause. "Toma said he was sleeping on the night Lirim was killed. By himself. He didn't feel well during the day and didn't make any of his usual runs for work. He's in the liquor distribution business. He said he stayed in all day, watched television by himself at night and then went to sleep."

"But Toma as the killer doesn't answer the two ligature question."

"No, unfortunately it doesn't," Gerry stifled a yawn.

"And if Toma did kill Lirim, why wait until Wednesday night? Why not do it on Tuesday night after he and Clara met Lirim at the elementary school?"

"Probably because Lirim wasn't in his trailer Tuesday night, Damon," Gerry snapped. He quickly apologized. "Sorry, I'm exhausted. Listen, Damon, I know you're just trying to help and I'm the one who brought you into this mess in the first place. But you're not a police officer and I can't have you acting like one."

"Gerry, I'm sorry," Damon said. "I never intended to jeopardize your investigation."

"I know you mean well, Damon. And you have gotten results, too, but enough is enough."

"Will you at least tell me where Lirim was on Tuesday night?"

Gerry groaned. "After Lirim and Victor left the Fish Barrel a week ago Tuesday, they took a taxi to a gentlemen's club in downtown D.C.," he said flatly. "After it closed, they spent a couple of hours at a late-night cigar bar. It was almost light outside by the time they arrived back at the fairgrounds. A few of the early risers saw them come in and retire to their separate trailers."

"Did you just find all of this out?" Damon asked.

"A short time ago, yes."

Damon contemplated the implications of Lirim and Victor going out on the town less than twelve hours after Toma threatened Lirim.

"Gerry," Damon said, "I should have called you before driving down to Richmond."

"Yes, and you shouldn't have called Johnnetta Frank. But it'll be all right. I'll take some shots from Margaret, but you've given us another solid lead. She recognizes that, and I'm fairly certain she won't mention it to the chief. In fact, she'll probably find a way for the department to take credit for it."

"Fine by me," Damon said with relief. "Are you going back to sleep or heading up to Baltimore?"

"I'll try to go back to sleep, but I'm sure I'll hear from the Baltimore city police within an hour about whether Toma Ljubic is at home."

"Will you let me know?" Damon asked, knowing he was pushing the envelope.

Gerry sighed. "Yes, Damon, I'll let you know."

It was just before two o'clock in the morning when Damon arrived at his duplex. He managed five hours of sleep and found a text message from Gerry waiting when he woke. "Toma's gone. We're questioning Clara. I'm going to Baltimore."

Damon felt his stomach turn. He knew that he shouldn't have spoken to Clara without talking to Gerry first. Because of him, Toma had vanished.

Chapter 20

Damon looked out of his bedroom window and considered the empty day ahead of him. He wasn't scheduled to go into the library and Bethany had cancelled their date for that night. It seemed like days since he played the message from Bethany, even though it had been just over twelve hours earlier.

Damon struggled internally. He wasn't sure whether he could do anything about Toma Ljubic, but he was desperate to try. Gerry had warned him to back away from the case and Damon knew he had made a serious mistake the night before. But his interest was far too deep to take a back seat now. Fueled by his discovery of the abuse of Hannah Roscoph, Damon's drive to track down Lirim's murderer overpowered him.

After a solid thirty minutes of forcing himself to stay put, and despite his better judgment, Damon gassed up the Saab and drove in the direction of Baltimore. He had put more miles on his car in the past week than in the previous two months.

Before leaving Arlington, Damon looked up Toma's address in the online white pages. It was just east of Charles Village. The village was stocked with local pubs and diners, which mingled with an eclectic mix of retro clothing stores. The neatly manicured lawns of Johns Hopkins' small but refined undergraduate campus bordered the western edge of Charles Village. But to the east lay seas of row houses that grew more bedraggled with each passing block.

Toma's address matched a two-story ramshackle, brown-brick structure on Greenmount Avenue. Damon parked along the curb a block down the street and walked toward the residence. A short flight of steps led to a stoop bereft of furnishing other than an orange clay flowerpot. Across the street, two men in plain clothes sat in a parked gray sedan. The man in the passenger street was focused on something in his lap, but the driver's eyes followed Damon as he walked. Poor cover if the policemen were trying to appear inconspicuous.

Damon didn't slow and continued north on foot. Three blocks from Toma's home, Damon saw a liquor store. In Virginia, hard liquor could only be purchased from a government-operated "ABC" store. Damon favored free-market capitalism because he believed competition brought down prices, but maybe cheaper vodka tonics weren't in the best interests of the state. Baltimore had privately-owned liquor markets, including "CHG on Greenmount," which was open on a weekday morning.

Damon stepped inside. The floor hadn't been swept and Damon felt grit crunch between his shoes and the linoleum. Alcohol bottles lined the shelves of two narrow aisles and a selection of inexpensive wines filled a third. The back of the store was reserved for commercial refrigerators stocked with malt liquor and beer. Security cameras hung from the ceiling, and a clear cage of bullet-resistant glass fronted a cashier who was perched behind a tiny counter. Damon couldn't fathom spending eight to ten hours a day in there, sliding money back and forth in a tray like a bank teller. The store was empty but for Damon and the cashier.

Damon approached him. "I was wondering if you know someone who lives around here."

The young Middle Eastern man behind the glass looked up from his crossword puzzle. "Who?"

"Toma Ljubic. He lives on Greenmount a few blocks down from here and he's a liquor distributor."

The man behind the glass surveyed Damon. "You don't look like you're with the police."

"Come again?" He had thrown Damon off guard.

"The police. They were in here the minute I opened up and asked the same question. I'll tell you the same thing I told them. I know who the guy is, but he doesn't sell here or to any of the liquor stores, just to restaurants and bars. He comes in and buys beer or wine every once in a while. What did he do?"

"What makes you think he did something?" Damon asked and realized the absurdity of the question before he finished speaking.

"The police come looking for the guy and less than an hour later you show up asking questions. What am I supposed to think?"

"Okay, sorry. Listen, I can't say what he may have done, but I need to find him."

"You need to find him before the police do?" the cashier asked, looking more interested.

Damon disappointed him. "No, I'm working with the police." It wasn't quite accurate but was closer to the truth than the alternative.

"Well, I haven't seen him in a little over a week. Try the local dives. I think he services most of them."

Damon muttered a thank you and exited. He retraced his steps back to the Saab and cruised the neighborhood, taking mental notes of the bars and restaurants, most of which opened at noon.

Once the lunch hour hit, Damon spent a solid two hours under a relentless sun ducking in and out of taverns, clubs and other eating and drinking establishments, peppering hostesses and bartenders with inquiries. The responses were mind-numbingly similar.

They knew Toma, but just as a salesperson, and hadn't seen him all day. Damon was careful to avoid a set of uniformed Baltimore City police officers asking similar questions. Even so, he envisioned the officers entering bar after bar and being told by countless wait staff that a tall clean-shaven man in a tan polo shirt had been asking similar questions only minutes earlier.

In an Irish pub he noticed a photocopied sketch of Toma left by the police lying on the rough wooden bar. He deftly swept it up and folded it into his front jeans pocket.

Three bars later, he hit an outer edge of Toma's route. A black-bearded bartender with a Medusa-inspired tattoo bulging beneath the taut rim of a shirt sleeve had never heard of Toma. A quick glance at the drawing didn't change his answer.

Damon decided to break there for lunch. It was after two in the afternoon, but the place was busy with late lunch-goers and a sprinkling of early drinkers. He spread out in a booth and ordered a French dip with curly fries and a soda.

Ten minutes into his meal, a teenage boy in a dirty busboy apron slid in across from Damon. "I overheard you talking to Jason at the bar about a guy named Toma," said the lanky dark-skinned kid without introduction.

Damon stopped chewing and swallowed hard. "Do you know him?"

"Let me see the picture you showed Jason."

Damon removed the wadded up sketch from his pocket and unfolded it on the table.

"I know him all right. His name's Toma but we all call him 'Grigor.' I'm not sure why. Some of the guys just started calling him that."

"What guys would those be?" Damon asked.

"Kids hanging around the block up near my house."

"Where's that?"

The teen stopped and eyed Damon more closely. "Are you a cop or something?"

"No. I just need to find Toma."

"How much is it worth to you?" he asked without lowering his voice.

"If you know where he is, you better tell me now. I'm not with the police, but the police are investigating him."

"Ah," he said. "So the cops *are* looking for him. I don't know exactly where he is, but unless he hopped a bus or train he can't be far."

Damon looked at the boy closely. He wasn't yanking Damon's chain. "Why do you say that? He has a car. I know he drove to the Washington, D.C., area just over a week ago."

"Either he just bought a car or that was a rental. My man Grigor goes everywhere on his bicycle. But he sold that last week, so the guy's on foot now."

Damon processed the information quickly. He reached into his back pocket and pulled out his wallet. It was bulging with two months' worth of cash register receipts. He had fifty three dollars in cash. Damon handed every bill to the busboy. "How do you know he sold his bicycle last week?"

The kid stuffed the wad of cash into the pocket of his apron. "Because I asked him and he told me. Grigor, I mean Toma, lives on the same block as me and some of my boys. He's an old guy, but we're all cool with him. Toma buys the hard stuff in bulk then he turns around and sells it at a mark-up."

The kid picked up three French fries from Damon's plate, dipped them in au jus and crammed them into his mouth. "Here's the thing," he said between chewing and swallowing. "The guy is lazy. He doesn't even pick up the bottles or deliver them. He has a buddy with a truck who does that. Toma says he has a warehouse somewhere in town, but he takes the bus when he needs to go there. The liquor companies deliver big shipments to his warehouse. Then his buddy takes a few bottles from each of the different companies, loads them in his truck and delivers them."

"Toma doesn't help?"

"Toma makes the deals. He talks to the liquor companies on the phone and goes to the bars and restaurants on his bicycle. I don't think he's at the warehouse too often because he's always hanging around on the streets. He drinks a lot, too."

"His own liquor?"

"Mostly. He gets it in bulk so it's pretty cheap. I think the only time he goes to the warehouse is to snag a few bottles for himself."

"And you and your buddies," Damon said.

"Maybe he does a little extra business on the side for some of the local kids," the busboy responded without concern. "A year or two ago, the police started raiding the liquor stores for selling to underage kids, so Toma's just filling a need."

"You're an economist?" Damon asked smiling.

"Something like that." The boy returned a grin.

"Let's get back to the bicycle," Damon said.

"I have to get back to work, man."

"I just paid you overtime. Give me five more minutes."

"Okay, but you have to leave a big tip for the waitress. She's starting to get lonely and is coming around to my charms."

Damon glanced at the waitress who was at least twice the busboy's age. Her meaty thighs weren't built for the tight skirt she was wearing. "Fine," he said. "How do you know Toma sold his bike, and who did he sell it to?"

"I told you, he told me he sold it. He almost always had it with him. Pretty nice looking, but I don't know anything about bicycles. I just know it was silver with a black seat. I saw Toma yesterday at about four o'clock. He didn't have the bike, and I hadn't seen him riding it for about a week. That was strange because he always rode it to the bars to take orders. I can't imagine a guy his age doing all of that on foot."

"So you asked him about the bike?"

"I asked him if it was in the shop. He said he was done with bikes because his knees were finally going out on him. He said he'd probably get a motor scooter."

"Did Toma say who he sold the bicycle to?" Damon asked.

"Nope. Just said he sold it."

"You haven't seen him around today, have you?"

"Not since yesterday afternoon when I asked him about the bike."

Damon let the youth get back to busing dishes and dunked a handful of sandwich into cold au jus, but laid it back on the plate. He fished out his phone, called Gerry and left him a message. He'd seen several police officers in the vicinity of Toma's row house that day, but hadn't seen Gerry. He abandoned his lunch and left the waitress a thirty percent tip on his credit card, just in case it could actually help the busboy get lucky.

Chapter 21

The tattooed bartender Jason only knew of one nearby location that might sell bicycles—a sporting goods store two miles to the northeast. Damon walked briskly back to his Saab. A gentle breeze lightened the sting of the July heat.

The shop was a local outfit rather than a national chain. Given its confined square footage in the city, parts and clothing were available for purchase but bicycles themselves were not. Damon showed the manager and two salesgirls Toma's picture for good measure, but all three shook their heads. The manager provided Damon with directions to a big-box sporting goods store just outside of the city, a specialty bicycle dealer and a place that bought and sold used sports equipment. The trade-in store sounded the most promising so Damon tried it first.

It was located in the urban suburb of Towson. A sizable showroom boasted new and used equipment for every athletic endeavor imaginable, but the carpet was worn to the slab and the lighting was low. In the mid-afternoon hour, customer traffic was light. Damon found his way to a section exhibiting an array of bicycles and a variety of parts and accessories that were largely unfamiliar to him.

A sprightly blond saleswoman bounded in his direction. She appraised him. "You're in pretty good shape, but I bet I can really get your heart pumping," she said with a twinkle in her eye.

Damon racked his brain for a witty rejoinder but couldn't bring one to his frontal lobe.

Saving him from mumbling out a lame response, the young saleswoman placed a hand on Damon's elbow. She guided him to wall of new bicycles mounted from floor to ceiling. "Do any of these strike your fancy, or are you looking for a used bike?"

Her cheeks glistened under light rouge, and glitter accentuated sea-green irises. She managed to make the look chic.

"I'm not looking for a bicycle," he said. "Well, actually I am."

The transformation of her facial expression from engaged to vacant was blatant as she presumably contemplated spending the next several minutes conversing with a meathead.

"Sorry," Damon said, quickly recovering his composure. "What I mean is I'm trying to find a man who sold a particular bicycle."

"Okay," she said cautiously. "Do you know the model?"

"I don't. I'm pretty certain it was silver with a black seat and it was sold within the past week to week and a half."

The blond cocked her head, waiting for more.

"I have a picture of the person who sold it," Damon said and showed her the paper bearing Toma Ljubic's visage.

She studied the image seriously for several seconds. "Are you sure he sold it here?"

Damon admitted that he wasn't.

She took a second look. "I don't recall seeing this person before, and I definitely didn't buy a used bike from him recently."

"Is there anyone else who might have purchased it?"

"The only other person who's authorized to buy bicycles is Teddy Vanover. And he's not working today."

Before Damon turned to leave, he spontaneously asked, "You wouldn't be interested in going out to dinner with me sometime, would you?"

"Sorry, sunshine, I'm married," she countered with a look that suggested she was pleased with herself.

She wasn't wearing a ring, which could be a tactic to facilitate sales. Or she may have just been making up a spouse to avoid a date without wounding Damon's ego.

He mumbled an apology and started to walk toward the exit.

She stepped quickly and caught up to him. "Hold on, you don't happen to have that guy's address do you?"

Damon stopped, fished Toma's address out of his wallet and passed it to her. "Do you think you can find him with this?"

"We'll see," she said, taking the slip of paper and stepping over to a computer terminal. After a few seconds of clattering keystrokes, she said, "Got him."

Damon moved closer. A primitive black screen with glowing green alphanumerics yielded basic but vital information. It listed Toma's home address, a short description of the bicycle model and purchase price. The screen also displayed a date of sale, which corresponded to the day after Lirim's murder. A comment read, "Shop: New chain and replace stiff brake cable."

"Teddy bought it," she said, pointing to his initials in a top corner of the display.

"Does 'Shop' mean it's in a repair shop somewhere?"

"It sure does. It's probably in the back right now."

Damon whistled. "I need to see it right now, and we need to get Teddy down here," he urged her.

"Hold on, cowboy," she said raising her hands. She was still smiling but stepped a pace back from Damon. His restlessness was palpable. "I've been patient and haven't asked you who you are or what you want with this bicycle. But now I think it's time for you to explain yourself."

Damon forced himself to take a deep breath. "I'm working with the police on an investigation, and I think the chain from that bicycle was part of the crime."

His attempt to leave out the gruesome details was futile—the blond was too shrewd. "Somebody got beaten with it, or killed," she said plainly.

She answered his unspoken question. "I can't think of any other crime where someone would use a bike chain. Was it murder?"

"I think so," he said. "I'm calling the police. Can you see if you can get Teddy to come to the store?"

"I'll try. First I have to go tell the manager."

Damon dialed Gerry. No answer. He left a voicemail and sent him both an e-mail and a text, providing the location of the sporting goods dealer. He tried Gerry's boss, Margaret Hobbes. Her voicemail box was full.

The blond sales clerk came back with a thumbs up, trailed by a Hispanic man in his early thirties who had love handles jutting out just above his belt. She introduced the manager as Jorge and divulged that her name was Gretchen. Jorge asked for a recap, which Damon provided succinctly.

"Are the police coming?" Jorge asked in unaccented rapid English.

"I called and texted them. I'm sure they'll be here soon. Is Teddy able to come in?"

"He'll be here in ten minutes," Jorge said. "He only lives a couple of miles away. He wasn't too pleased to get a call from me on his day off, but when I said he may have bought a bike from a murderer, he got pretty excited."

"Can we take a look at the bike while we wait?" Damon asked.

"I don't see why not," Jorge said. Gretchen returned to the computer and printed out a screen shot of Toma's sale.

The storage area was a cemetery for discarded sports equipment. Exercise bicycles and weightlifting benches dominated the front of the room. The sides were lined with wheeled bins overflowing with loose gear—everything from wooden tennis rackets to snowshoes.

At the back of the storage room a set of doors led to a rectangular cement block workshop. A twenty-something man with corn-rows, dirty jeans and bright white Nikes was sitting on a low work table restringing the pocket of a lacrosse stick. "Hey boss," he said upon seeing Jorge walk into the windowless space.

"Gene," Jorge said, "I need you to find a bike for me." Gretchen handed him the slip of paper.

He peered down at it and stepped over to a metallic rack housing a half-dozen bicycles. Gene pulled out a silver bike with a black seat, just as the busboy had described.

"It's the next bike on my list," Gene said.

"So you haven't touched it?" Damon asked quickly.

"I've moved it around a few times, but I haven't worked on it yet."

"And it didn't have a chain when it came in?" Gretchen asked, her eyes wide with anticipation.

"Not that I saw," Gene said. "I think Teddy brought it back a little over a week ago. And he wouldn't have taken off the chain. Why all the questions, Jorge?"

"It might be part of a police investigation," Jorge responded cryptically.

"You want me to do anything in particular with it?"

"Just leave it as is for now. Don't repair it please."

"No problem, boss," Gene said, revealing braces on his teeth.

Minutes later, a well-built Caucasian man bustled through the doors of the workshop.

"Are the police here?" he asked loudly.

Jorge introduced him to Damon. Teddy Vanover had the classic "V" shape of a bodybuilder. His shoulders were expansive and his torso tapered evenly down to a narrow waist. He wore a tight yellow t-shirt and black mesh shorts. Damon was surprised the store had him working in the bicycle department rather than the weightlifting section.

Damon quickly filled in Teddy on the background and then asked if he remembered the person who sold him the chainless bicycle.

"I think so. He was an older guy, bald in front but with long hair in the back.

Damon unfolded the photocopy and handed it to Teddy.

He responded immediately. "That's him."

"You're sure?" Damon asked.

"Definitely."

"And the bike didn't have a chain on it when he brought it in?"

"It didn't. I'm pretty sure I wrote that in the computer report."

"Did he buy anything in exchange?" Jorge asked.

"No," Teddy said. "I just wrote out a receipt for the purchase and he said he'd be back later to use the credit."

A girl of no more than nineteen poked her head through the workshop door. Her face was flush with anxiety, but it mellowed when she spotted Jorge. "Jorge," she whispered. "The police are here."

"Good," he said. "Bring them back here right away."

Within a matter of seconds, Margaret Hobbes, Gerry Sloman and two Baltimore police officers crowded into the workshop. Damon, Gretchen and Jorge were asked to step outside of the tight space but to stay on the premises. The officers needed breathing room while they questioned Teddy and Gene.

Damon joined Gretchen outside for a breath of fresh air while Jorge returned to his managerial duties.

"What a trip," she said. "Do you have a cigarette?"

"I don't smoke, sorry," Damon responded, wondering why he had apologized.

"Neither do I," she said. "Not normally, anyway. But this is crazy."

A trio of women parked their bicycles against the rack in front of the store. Gretchen whispered an expletive and excused herself—the bicycle sales section had been unstaffed for half an hour. Damon sat on the concrete walkway separating the parking lot from the store. Forty-five minutes later, one of the Baltimore police officers asked him to step inside.

Gerry was waiting for him in the storage area. Margaret was still in the workshop. Damon expected to be chewed out for interfering yet again, but instead Gerry slapped him on the back. "Terrific work, Damon. The department owes you one."

"No problem," Damon said, unsure whether the compliment was genuine.

"Seriously, Damon. Margaret was upset about you talking to Clara alone, and she's pissed off that Toma's running loose, but you found rock-solid evidence for Lirim's murder and that means a whole lot."

"Thanks." Damon lowered his voice. "Gerry, the chain was used after the clothesline. So Toma isn't the murderer, is he?"

"We'll see. Maybe he'll crack under interrogation or maybe the prosecutor's office will come up with a winning theory as to why the chain was involved in the actual death."

"Would they do that even if Dr. Chu said he was already dead by the time he was strangled with the chain?"

"I don't know. At the very least, we should be able to get him for attempted murder. If you can attempt to murder a dead man. But we'll let the prosecutor's office work that out."

"Do you have enough evidence?" Damon asked.

"I think so. We have a strong motive. Toma just found out crucial information supporting what he may have long suspected—that Lirim killed his sister. He has no alibi. And the day after Lirim was strangled with a bicycle chain, he sells a bicycle that doesn't have a chain. Margaret's getting the physical specifications of the standard chain for Toma's model so we can confirm that they match the marks found on the body. But they'll match, I'm certain."

Chapter 22

The specifications of the missing chain corresponded to a tee to the marks found on Lirim's neck. Gerry e-mailed Damon with the information that evening after Damon had driven home to Hollydale. Gerry had other news as well. Police in Newark, New Jersey, tracked down and arrested Toma Ljubic, who was being transported to Arlington. He was found with an overnight bag stuffed full of cash at a YMCA within walking distance of a commercial bus depot.

The following day was Saturday. Damon took a morning walk to The Cookery. He wanted to find out if Rebecca and his mother enjoyed the show at the Kennedy Center.

Lights were on, but the cooking school was empty. Next door at Cynthia's salon, through the plate glass window, Damon observed a small pack of women buzzing around Mrs. Chenworth. He recognized Rebecca from the rear.

"Is everything all right?" Damon asked, stepping inside.

All heads turned in his direction.

"Mrs. Chenworth slipped crossing the street from the Safeway," Cynthia said. A sly smile on her emaciated face suggested they were feeding the large woman's frenzy out of benevolence. Her health and welfare were hardly at risk.

"Thank goodness the cars were stopped at the light," Mrs. Chenworth said to Damon, pleased to find a new pair of sympathetic ears. "Though I suppose that's why

I was crossing. But still, I stepped right in a crack in the middle of the street. Damon, you're in charge of Hollydale, can't you do something about it?"

"I'll see what I can do," he responded in an overly serious tone and Rebecca gave him a quick wink. "Did you call an ambulance?"

"No, no," Mrs. Chenworth said with a wave of her hand. "Rebecca came to my rescue. I'm injured, of course, but I can live without the hospital. Don't get me started on that place. Say, Damon, what's happening in the murder case?"

"The police in Newark arrested someone last night and are bringing him back to Arlington for questioning," he said, leaning back against a spotless countertop.

"Who?" Mrs. Chenworth nearly leapt out of her chair. Rebecca had to cover her mouth to avoid laughing at the dynamism of the wounded woman.

Damon debated how much to disclose to an audience that included the gossipy Mrs. Chenworth. "The police arrested the dead man's brother-in-law," Damon said.

"It's always family in these cases," pontificated Mrs. Chenworth easing back into the comfort of the salon styling chair. "What's the motive?"

Damon deftly parried away the question by describing his encounter with the murder suspect. "Do you remember last week when you told me that Lirim's daughter and her doctor boyfriend were headed to the Poorboy Diner?"

"Yes," she responded excitedly.

"That's where I met the man who was arrested."

Mrs. Chenworth radiated with delight. Damon concluded she was devising a story that led from her giving Jordan Hall directions to a diner to the capture of a murderer.

"Well, it looks like you're feeling better, Mrs. Chenworth," Damon said cutting short the dialogue. "Rebecca needs me to help her fix something at The Cookery."

Rebecca followed his lead and the pair extricated themselves from the rumormonger and her cohorts.

The rich smell of freshly ground Kona beans filled the air in The Cookery as Rebecca brewed coffee in a French press.

"So what really happened?" she asked.

Damon relayed Victor's story about Lirim murdering his wife and then outlined his call to Johnnetta Frank and the trip to Richmond. He used general terms to describe his day in Baltimore, leaving out all mention of Toma's bicycle. As far as Rebecca knew, a nylon clothesline was the only weapon used on Lirim.

"Do you know what the police found to pin down Toma?" she asked when he finished his account.

Damon hesitated. "I do. I just can't tell you."

She took it in stride. "No problem, Damon."

Damon hesitated and Rebecca homed in on his disquiet. "Why aren't you happier?" she asked. "Lirim was a scumbag and now there's some closure for the citizens of Hollydale."

Damon avoided her gaze. "I can't tell you why, but the case isn't over yet," he said.

She was clearly puzzled but not upset with Damon. She didn't want him to say anything he wasn't comfortable disclosing.

"So what happens next?" she asked.

"The police will grill Toma. And I'll wait and hope that Gerry throws me some scraps."

Walking toward home, up the base of the hill separating Hollydale's commercial district from its residential streets, Damon noticed Skipper at a table outside of the Baskin Robbins with Shawna Crane, the local girl Skipper met at the fair. He wondered what Skipper was doing in Hollydale on a Saturday morning when the fair in Manassas would be in full swing.

Damon crossed over to the couple. Skipper smiled, stood up and extended his hand. Not the gesture of someone hiding a terrible secret.

"Will you join us for a scoop, Mr. Lassard?"

"No thanks, Skipper. Hi Shawna. I was just heading home and wanted to say hello. Are you playing hooky today, Skipper?"

"No. Jim let me take off this morning to see Shawna. Manassas is close enough that we've been able to see each other every day. But next week Big Surf is heading out to Cumberland. That's two and a half hours from here, so it could be a whole week before I see Shawna again."

Damon liked Skipper when he first met him and his opinion hadn't changed. He wished them both good luck and continued on foot up the hill to his duplex.

David Einstaff was not on the porch. That was a good sign. He might be at work rather than enjoying life somewhere, but at least he wasn't drunk on the porch on a Saturday before noon.

The reminder of the day passed uneventfully. Damon popped into the branch library to see if he could catch Bethany who was a frequent library visitor. She wasn't there and he chastised himself for looking. He hadn't seen her since the Fourth of July picnic and was sure she was avoiding him.

Chapter 23

At seven-thirty the next evening Gerry called. "We did it, Damon!" he shouted into the telephone. "It's over. We brought Toma in to the station and he came clean. We have more physical evidence, too. Come by and I'll let you listen to the tape." Damon pumped a fist in the air and told Gerry he'd be right over. He found a bottle of expensive champagne that had been collecting dust and sped over to the Sloman residence.

Trina greeted Damon with a peck on the cheek and led him into Gerry's study. Brown wainscoting darkened the room. A small desk and two deep green fabric armchairs crowded the small space. Gerry shook Damon's hand vigorously, then pulled him into a brief embrace.

"Congratulations, Gerry," Damon said. "I knew your hard work would pay off."

"Thanks to you, Damon." He accepted the champagne and poured Damon a glass of wine from an open bottle. "Trina and I had a celebratory glass earlier," he explained.

"You said he came clean. So Toma was the murderer after all?"

"Actually no. Listen to the tape and you can hear the same thing I did."

Gerry walked over to a cassette player. Damon wondered when the police department would upgrade its technology.

"Toma didn't resist arrest when the Newark police picked him up," Gerry said. "He said he was on his way to visit a friend in Connecticut and just stopped in New Jersey to spend the night. It probably isn't true, but it doesn't matter." His finger hovered over the play button. "I have it set up to start after we conducted all of the formalities. So what you're hearing is Margaret Hobbes with Toma. I'm in the room as well, but I'm just there to look scary."

The two men exchanged smiles. In spite of Gerry's detection skills, intimidation was simply not in his arsenal. "A court appointed defense lawyer is in the room as well," Gerry continued. "But he looked like he graduated from law school yesterday. He barely spoke."

"A bit of luck," Damon said and sat down.

"Perhaps, but after you hear what's on the tape, you'll see that a good defense lawyer would probably have advised Toma to tell us everything."

Gerry pushed play and Margaret's voice filled the room.

"We found your bicycle, Mr. Ljubic. The clerk of the sporting goods store in Towson confirmed that you sold it to him the day after you murdered Lirim Jovanović. Without a chain."

Silence filled the air while Margaret Hobbes waited for Toma to speak. He didn't.

"Mr. Ljubic, the salesman you sold the bicycle to positively identified you. In addition, forensic evidence clearly shows that the chain used to strangle Lirim Jovanović was the standard model for your bicycle."

Toma winced audibly. "Maybe I changed the chain a year ago to a different model," he said with an air of desperation. His voice was guttural.

Margaret pounced at him, her voice rising. "Are you telling me, Mr. Ljubic, that you *did* change the chain on your bicycle a year ago? And remember, if you're not truthful, we'll tack on an obstruction of justice charge so fast it'll make your head spin."

There was another pause. "So, Mr. Ljubic, did you or did you not change the chain on your bike?" she repeated.

"I didn't," he said quietly. "But I bought it used, so maybe the previous owner changed it."

Margaret let the comment pass. "So, you sold Mr. Vanover your chainless bicycle the day after the murder and the chain marks around the dead man's neck match the chain model standard to that very bicycle," Margaret summarized. "In addition, Mr. Ljubic, your niece, Clara Jovanović, gave us a statement. She informed us of the conversation you two had with your brother-in-law the day before he was killed. Stop me if this doesn't sound familiar. You previously suspected that your brother-in-law was involved in your sister Tabby's death, but you didn't know for sure. Then a week ago Tuesday, Clara told you that Lirim had taken photos of a young girl a number of years ago. In addition, Clara told you that Tabby not only found the pictures but she confronted Lirim just before she died. That was enough for you to decide that Lirim killed your sister and you wanted him dead."

Toma didn't respond.

Margaret continued. "And the police have learned, Mr. Ljubic, that your suspicions were correct. Lirim Jovanović did indeed murder your sister."

Damon pictured Toma breaking into a smile at the news, which would sweep away any reservations he had about strangling Lirim.

"Good," muttered Toma.

"If you look at the evidence," Margaret said, "you can see that no jury in the world will acquit you." Of course, she left out the part about the other set of strangulation marks which the autopsy indicated delivered the death blow.

Toma asked if he could take a cigarette break and Margaret said no. He requested a glass of water, which Gerry fetched. Upon Gerry's return, Toma started to speak.

"Okay," Toma said, "I was in Lirim's trailer, but I didn't kill him and I can prove it."

"When were you there, Mr. Ljubic? On the night of his murder?"

"Yes, and the night before." He took a drink of water. "The night before he was killed, his trailer was empty and I waited for three or four hours, but he never arrived."

Margaret's voice cut in. "Were you waiting in his trailer?"

"I was. It was unlocked. I went in after midnight and he wasn't there so I waited. He never came in so I left before the sun came up." Damon knew Lirim had been with Victor at the gentlemen's club and cigar bar all night.

Toma coughed. "I came back the following night. There was a group of kids having a bonfire and drinking. I parked on the street a few blocks away from the school and found a spot in the woods where I could see the backs of the trailers. At about a quarter after midnight, Lirim came out of his trailer and broke up the bonfire. His light went off fifteen minutes later. I planned to go in at two thirty in the morning when he would be sure to be asleep. But that didn't happen."

Toma stopped and Damon could hear him crunching ice between his teeth. There were quiet mumblings which Gerry said was the defense attorney whispering something to Toma and Toma cursing at him in return. "After that, the lawyer didn't say another word," Gerry explained to Damon and refilled both of their wine glasses. Damon arched his back to give it a good stretch. Gerry's home was silent but for the sound of the recording.

"Please continue, Mr. Ljubic," Margaret said.

"About an hour after the lights went out in Lirim's trailer, I heard noises. It was dark and the school lights didn't reach that part of the fairgrounds, but the moon was bright and my eyes had adjusted by then. I saw a man come out of the next mobile home over."

Gerry gave Damon a double thumbs up as Margaret asked, "You mean the trailer right beside Lirim's?"

"Yes."

"Could you identify the person?"

"Not then, but later I could. Let me get to that."

"Okay, please go on."

"He was carrying a grocery bag. Just a brown paper one with the top folded over. He walked around the far end of his mobile home and disappeared from my view for about thirty seconds. Then he reentered my sight line and stepped into Lirim's motor home without knocking. He was only in there for two minutes or so. I couldn't hear anything and no one turned on the lights. At the time, I thought they must be whispering. After the man came back out I thought he'd reenter his mobile home but he didn't. He carried the grocery bag up the hill to the playground at the school."

"Were the lights on at the playground?" Margaret inquired.

"Yes. I tracked him through the woods. I was wearing soft-soled shoes and there weren't any leaves on the ground so I was able to be pretty quiet. I don't think he heard me. He never turned to look toward the woods."

"Is that when you recognized him?" Margaret asked firmly. "Under the lights at the playground?"

"It was. It was Lirim's accountant Victor. I tried to steer clear of Lirim as a general rule, despite being related to him through marriage. But it seemed like every time I saw Lirim, Victor was with him. So I knew the man by sight."

"Victor McElroy?" Margaret said to clarify for the recorder.

"Yes, that's him."

On the recording, Damon could hear Margaret Hobbes asking Gerry to produce the Front Royal mug shot and Toma confirming Victor was the man he saw emerge from Lirim's trailer at approximately one thirty in the morning on the day of Lirim's murder. Margaret asked Toma to proceed.

"Victor got down on his knees and started digging with his hands on the underside of a green plastic slide. The playground's base is mulch, so he took off the gloves he was wearing and dug in quickly. After he made a decent sized hole, he put the gloves back on, shoved the paper bag in the hole and covered it with mulch."

"And what did you think he was doing?" Margaret asked.

"I thought that he and Lirim were involved in a narcotics sale. I figured the bag contained either money or drugs and he was hiding it so the people he shared his mobile home with wouldn't find it. Or maybe he was a middleman and the playground slide was a pre-planned drop site for someone else to come along later and dig it out."

"But Victor and Lirim were alone almost every day," Margaret said, playing devil's advocate. "Why wait until the middle of the night to make an exchange and why wear gloves?"

"I didn't think about it at the time, and I don't know if he had on gloves when he went into Lirim's trailer.

But if it had been a drug deal, Victor couldn't be burying paper bags in the broad daylight. It doesn't matter—they weren't making an exchange."

"So there weren't drugs in the paper bag?"

"No." He paused to instill his own effect. "Or cash. After he buried the bag, Victor returned to his motor home. I waited another two hours before doing anything. I assumed it would take some time for Lirim to fall back asleep after conducting his business with Victor, and I wanted to make sure no one else was coming to dig under the slide."

"So you didn't dig up the bag after Victor went back inside?"

"Not right away. I was too focused on Lirim. And if someone else came to dig up the bag and it wasn't there, he might have tromped down to the fairgrounds and started knocking on doors and I didn't want that happening."

"Because you didn't want to be interrupted while you were strangling Lirim," Margaret said.

Toma ignored the jab. "At three forty five in the morning, I went into Lirim's motor home. I had the bicycle chain with me. My eyes had adjusted to the night sky outside but the inside of the mobile home was even darker. Lirim's bedroom was almost pitch black. I didn't waste any time. I had gloves on and felt a foot at the near end of the bed so I moved quickly to the other end, wrapped the chain around the front of his neck and pulled up. The problem was, lieutenant, he didn't resist at all."

Margaret didn't respond, so Toma kept speaking. "Lirim Jovanović was dead when I tried to strangle him. His head and neck were totally slack. When I had touched his foot, I had gloves on and I think he had socks on, so I didn't feel that it had gone cold. I wrapped the chain around his neck and jerked up so fast that I didn't realize until after I started pulling that the man was already dead. I swear to it. I may have tried to kill him, but I didn't kill him."

"That's quite a story, Mr. Ljubic," Margaret said. "It sounds like a last ditch plea from a murderer trying to get by with a lesser crime."

"It's the truth and I can prove it."

"You said that before. We certainly want to hear how, but first tell me why you didn't tell us this story until now. It would have saved a whole lot of police effort if you had. And looked a lot better for you."

Damon could hear ruffling noises as if Toma was shifting in his chair. Gruffness returned to his voice. "Just because I didn't kill him, I know I'm not walking out of here a free man. I knew that if I told the truth I'd be going to jail. So I wasn't going to tell the police unless I had to. Well, now that you found the bicycle and found out about that asshole killing my sister, I'm in a different position, aren't I?"

Margaret answered. "You certainly are. Let's hear your so-called proof."

"I have the bag Victor buried in the playground," Toma said and laughed. "After I realized Lirim was dead, it occurred to me that Victor must have killed him. So I decided to see what he hid under the slide. I dug it up and then took it to my car before I even opened it."

"I have sources who say you don't own a car, Mr. Ljubic," Margaret said.

"It was a rental. A black compact car. I'm sure I can find the receipt if you need it."

Margaret didn't respond.

Toma continued. "I got in the car and drove about five miles to an empty parking lot at a strip mall. I looked in the bag and found two things. A pair of shearing scissors and a three-foot length of clothesline."

"Did you touch the objects with your bare hands?"

"No way. I kept my gloves on the whole time, even while I was driving. I don't think my bare hands ever even touched the paper bag."

"So let me ask you this, Mr. Ljubic," Margaret said. "If Victor McElroy was also wearing gloves when he handled those items, how do we know that he, and not you, used the shears to cut the clothesline and choke Lirim?"

The question threw Toma into a rage and he started shouting obscenities at Margaret.

Gerry pressed the stop button.

Damon stood and rolled his neck in a circle. "If things happened as Toma described, that would explain the multiple ligature marks and the timing of them."

"I know," Gerry replied. "And so did Margaret. She wanted to scare him and she can be a little vindictive at times. But it was a valid question."

"Can you play the rest of the tape? I want to hear his answer."

"There's not much more. The gist of Toma's tirade is that the police are idiots and the system is corrupt if we can't convict Victor based on his statement and finding the murder weapon."

"Did Toma still have the paper bag?" Damon asked.

"He did. Later, after we calmed him down, he pinpointed the location for us. The bag was in a desk drawer at his liquor distribution warehouse. The Baltimore police retrieved the bag for us yesterday afternoon. Toma said he saved it as a bargaining chip. He figured he'd need it if the police arrested him so he could point a finger at Victor. He also wanted to keep it in case Victor approached him—he thought he might need it to save his life."

"If Victor tried to dig up the bag after the police left the crime scene, I can only imagine how freaked out he must have been when he found that it had disappeared."

"No kidding," Gerry said. "He must have gone crazy. If not for Toma, it would have been a good move on Victor's part to hide the bag. He couldn't take it too far away because every extra minute he was out of his own trailer, he risked one of his bunkmates waking up and noticing that he was missing. But he had to assume that the police would search every trailer on the premises so he couldn't hide it in there."

"So it would have worked if Toma hadn't seen him."

"Possibly. We searched the playground and everywhere else in the vicinity of the fairgrounds for evidence, but we weren't digging holes."

"Toma didn't say that he saw Victor cut the clothesline. Did he say it off of the recording?"

"Margaret asked. He said he didn't see Victor cut a cord. But based on where the clothesline was kept, Margaret and I think Victor cut it during the thirty seconds he was out of Toma's line of sight—right before entering Lirim's trailer."

"I assume the paper bag still had the shears and clothesline in it."

"It did—a pair of very distinctive heavy-duty electrician's shears with red vinyl handles and a three-foot length of nylon clothesline. Our lab techs are fast-tracking the analysis. We're still waiting for official confirmation, but the unofficial news is tremendous."

"Should I open the champagne?" Damon asked.

"Now's as good a time as any," Gerry replied. "But just one glass. I want to stay lucid."

Damon popped the cork and poured the bubbly over the dregs at the bottom of their wine glasses.

"The shears still had particles of the clothesline attached to the blades so we know that those shears cut the ligature," Gerry said. "And the three-foot length of nylon cord visually matches the clothesline we collected from the fairgrounds over a week ago. Of course, the lab will confirm all of this, but I have no doubt."

"That's great," Damon said.

"But that's not the best part. I snapped some digital photos of the shears, and Margaret and I took them to the Big Surf folks in Manassas last night. We individually pulled aside ten full-time carnival workers, including the three who shared a trailer with Victor, and showed them the photos. We asked if they had seen the shears before. And if so, where."

"They were Victor's?"

"You got it. All three of his trailer mates and six of the other seven immediately said they were Victor's shears. He kept them with his personal gear and used them for odd jobs around the carnival."

"What about the one who didn't recognize the shears?"

"She looked nervous. She probably put two and two together and decided lying to the police was safer than pointing a finger at Victor. Either way, we have more than enough to sic the prosecutor on him."

"Are you going to bring him back to Arlington for trial?"

"Definitely," Gerry said. "We'll try him on Lirim's murder here. The attorneys will figure out all of the charges and then decide in what order to bring them. I'm sure he'll stand trial both here and in West Virginia."

Gerry excused himself and went to check on Trina. Damon felt bad for her. Gerry had been working around the clock for a week and a half and when he finally had a bit of respite, Damon was monopolizing his time. But

Gerry had invited him over. And they had unofficially worked hand-in-hand to solve the case.

Gerry returned and left his study door cracked open.

"Is everything okay?" Damon asked.

"It couldn't be better. I just wanted to give Trina a kiss and thank her again for being so understanding of my recent work schedule."

Damon was sure it had been difficult for her, not only to be apart from her husband but also to stay strong knowing that he was searching for a murderer.

"Do you think Victor will confess now that you have the weapon?" Damon asked.

"I can say with almost absolute certainty that he won't. Margaret and I drove out to West Virginia at five o'clock this morning. She took another shot at Victor."

Gerry certainly had been busy. He had spent at least seven hours in a car today driving to Morgantown and back.

"He didn't admit to anything?" Damon asked.

"Not a thing, but we don't need a statement to convict him." Gerry sat back down and pressed his hands against his thighs. "In fact, he didn't say a word. Between the time we questioned him about Hannah Roscoph and today, he found a lawyer. The defense attorney instructed him not to say anything."

"That's pretty common, right?"

"It is. And the lawyer needs time to figure out what exactly his client has done. Victor's looking at charges of accessory to kidnapping, child abuse, accessory to distribution of child pornography, first degree murder on Lirim and possibly even a charge of accessory to murder for Tabby's death."

Damon held out his fist and Gerry gave it a mild-mannered bump with his own.

"Do you think Victor was trying to keep Lirim from implicating him in Tabby's death?" Damon asked.

"I'd put my money on it," Gerry said. "Assuming Clara can be believed, when Lirim met Toma and Clara on the elementary school playground the day before the murder, Victor was watching from the woods. Lirim probably asked Victor to spy just in case things got rough and he needed back-up. Victor may not have been able to hear the conversation, but he saw Toma push Lirim and get in his face so he knew something was happening."

"And that's why Lirim and Victor went to downtown D.C. that same night," Damon interjected. "To discuss the situation."

"That's what Margaret and I think—Lirim told Victor that Toma and Clara knew about the pictures and they suspected Lirim in Tabby's death. If Toma or Clara told the authorities in West Virginia that Tabby not only found the pictures but found them right before her 'accident,' Lirim would be in a bind. Sheriff Anbani would have enough ammunition to reopen the case and investigate Lirim with full force. If Anbani was able to implicate Lirim in Tabby's death, then Lirim could turn on Victor if he played a part in Tabby's murder or cover-up."

"Lirim would have brought down Victor to get a plea bargain," Damon said.

"Exactly. So Victor killed Lirim to eliminate all connection between him and Tabby."

"Other than the paint from his truck."

"Yes," Gerry said. "But if the paint was all a prosecutor had, it would have been impossible to convict Victor for Tabby's death. Especially if he stuck to his story that he was well over a hundred miles away on the night she died."

Damon stood and leaned against the desk. "Will you be able to prove that Victor was in Morgantown when Tabby was killed?" he asked.

"I'm not sure whether the prosecutor will have enough circumstantial evidence to convince a jury. But even if it doesn't stick in court, Victor will never see daylight again anyway after he's convicted on Lirim's murder and the charges involving Hannah Roscoph. Still, Margaret and I spent the entire return drive from Morgantown today discussing why Victor would help Lirim kill Tabby."

Damon looked at Gerry with interest.

"Two possibilities," Gerry said. "One is that Lirim paid him to help. Tabby didn't change her will before she died, so Lirim received about one hundred and fifty thousand dollars. He could have given Victor a share of that money. The other reason is that Lirim probably told Tabby that Victor served as the cameraman in Hannah Roscoph's photo shoot. So Victor had an incentive to silence Tabby as well. Even though she told Lirim she didn't want to tell the police, Victor couldn't be sure she wouldn't change her mind."

"Sounds right to me." Damon paused. "You must be exhausted, Gerry."

"I am," he said, rising to his feet. "I'm taking a week's vacation, and Trina and I are headed to the beach at Ocean City."

Damon congratulated Gerry again before departing and whispered into Trina's ear as she hugged him goodbye at the door, "Make sure he rests for real while you're away."

Chapter 24

Damon decided to walk home even though Gerry lived a half mile from Damon's duplex. He had drunk enough wine and champagne to feel the effects—he could fetch his car in the morning.

The nighttime air was clammy and after several minutes, perspiration began to drip from his brow. He looked at his watch when he passed by his mother's townhouse. It was just before eleven but the lights were still on.

He knocked and within seconds Lynne Lassard-Brown opened the door and laughed. "I knew this would happen." She called over her shoulder, "Rebecca, we're caught in the act."

Damon followed his mother inside and saw Rebecca on the sitting room love seat holding a cup and saucer. She was wedged between two large cardboard boxes overflowing with clothing. Lynne took a seat on a chair that normally resided in the dining room.

"Your mother invited me over for a cup of tea," Rebecca explained before Damon could question her presence. She rose to her feet. "You look like you need a comfortable seat, Damon. I'll get another chair from the dining room."

Damon held up a hand. "How about I move these boxes, and we can sit together like civilized people," he said and cleared them away.

"Cup of tea?" asked his mother.

"No thanks. Since when do you invite my friends over?"

"Since never," Lynne responded. "But Rebecca and I had a good time the other night at the Kennedy Center and I thought it would be nice for us to get together again. I called you, too."

"Sorry, I was over at Gerry's," Damon said.

Rebecca leaned forward. "Anything new with the case?"

Damon exhaled. "It's over." He gave the two women in his life a truncated description of the final turns of the murder investigation. Damon was finally able to clue Rebecca in to the fact that the police found evidence of two separate strangulations.

"It makes so much more sense now," Rebecca said. "After you told me the police arrested Toma but the case wasn't over, I have to admit I was frustrated. Not with you, Damon, but I couldn't piece the story together because I didn't have the full picture."

"I can imagine how aggravating that must have been," Damon said.

Lynne Lassard-Brown smiled. "I hope this means that poor girl in California won't have to testify and go through her living hell again."

"I hope not, either," Damon said. "Gerry thinks Victor will be tried here for murder and in West Virginia on the charges involving the girl. If he's convicted in Arlington first, maybe the West Virginia prosecutors will show some mercy and conduct the trial out there without her live testimony. They have the recording that the Morgantown sheriff made."

"At least some good came out if this," Rebecca said. "Not only does she get closure, but so does your new sheriff friend in West Virginia."

"True," Damon responded, making a mental note to call Ravi Anbani the following day to congratulate him. "And Gerry solved his first murder case. I know he's thrilled."

"With a little help from you," he mother chimed in.

"Very little," Damon said with as much humility as he could muster. "I'm going to head home now. It's been a long night."

"Maybe you can walk Rebecca home," Lynne said.

"Sure. Are you ready, Rebecca?"

"Just let me just put my tea cup in the sink," she said and weaved her way through Lynne's clutter to the back of the narrow townhouse.

Damon grinned at his mother and shook his head.

"Can't blame me for trying," she said and kissed him on the forehead.

After a brisk walk in a comfortable silence, Damon declined Rebecca's invitation inside for a drink. He watched her disappear behind the front door and wondered yet again if he should capitulate and start dating Rebecca.

Damon weighed the pros and cons as he set off down the sidewalk toward his duplex and pulled the phone from his pocket. He had turned the ringer off when Gerry started to play back the recording of Toma Ljubic. There was a message waiting. He pressed a button on the keypad and Bethany's voice filled his ear.

"Hi Damon. It's Bethany. I'm sorry about cancelling the other night. Give me a call and let's get together and do something soon."

Damon smiled, shook his head in confusion, then smiled again as he walked home.

ABOUT THE AUTHOR

STEPHEN KAMINSKI is the author of *It Takes Two to Strangle*, the first book in the Damon Lassard Dabbling  Detective series. He is a graduate of Johns Hopkins University and Harvard Law School. Stephen has practiced law for well over a decade and currently serves as General Counsel to a national non-profit organization. He is a lifelong lover of all types of mysteries, including cozies, and lives with his wife and daughter in Arlington, Virginia.

www.ingramcontent.com/pod-product-compliance
Lightning Source LLC
Chambersburg PA
CBHW020313260626
47156CB00004B/1202